I0699646

THE PROFESSIONAL WIFE

ALSO BY MARYANN REID

Sex and the Single Sister

Use Me or Lose Me

Marry Your Baby Daddy

Mrs. Big

Every Man For Herself

This Life

THE PROFESSIONAL WIFE

A NOVEL

MARYANN REID

ALPHANISTA BOOKS

Hardback: ISBN 979-8-218-07696-2

Ebook: ISBN 979-8-218-07754-9

Paperback: ISBN 979-8-218-07755-6

Published by Alphanista® Books LLC

Printed in the United States of America

First Edition

 Created with Vellum

For my mother, my angel, my home

ACKNOWLEDGMENTS

It always feels like I am starting over with each book. Well, this one has been on the docket since 2016. With the help of editors, designers, agents, and the like, I finished it. I thank my mother, Veronica Reid, for being the mother I needed. Without her, and God, I wouldn't be alive today. May she rest in peace.

Thank you to Pastor Sherri & Pastor Tommy, Ms. Roberta, and all the prayer warriors who prayed for me when I knew and didn't know. Thank you to friends who echoed my mom's voice and always asked when my next book was coming out. That kept me going.

Thank you to Josephine Baker, Celia Cruz, Maya Angelou, Zora Neale Hurston, Pat Cleveland, Grace Jones, Tina Turner, who dared to live colorful and vibrant lives.

Thank you to the *Maryann Reid VIP Reader Group* on Facebook for cheering me on as I put this book together, and for all your support.

Thank you Jesus. Your name is above every name.

Guarded and guided.

PROLOGUE

The breeze gently lifted the delicate lace off her sun-kissed shoulders, and she shivered with excitement. Beyond the lush gardens before her, vineyards wound for acres upon acres with different varietals of grapes. They'd chosen this vineyard in Napa for the wedding after a very romantic weekend shortly after they started dating. The grounds were stunning, a hundred shades of green against the baby-blue sky. The evening they had planned for the celebration was over-the-top but elegant, and with the rustic backdrop, it was perfect. Candy couldn't imagine getting married anywhere else.

Cleveland Rogers III took her hand, and with a twinkle in his eye, he began his vows.

"I, Cleveland Rogers III, take you, Candy Miller Robertson, as my wife, to have ..."

Cleveland looked dashing in his black Armani tux, with a black satin bowtie and a stiffly ironed pocket square. He was undeniably handsome—tall and broad, smooth chocolate skin, and shining dark eyes—but he had more than just good looks. He was charming, effusive even. And she loved that she could read the emotions on his face so clearly. She never had to worry what he was thinking. They'd both been pampered and plucked at the spa the day before, and now she appreciated all of the effort. His hands were smooth and firm, and his skin seemed to radiate.

Candy remembered when they first met six months ago like it was yesterday, which, granted, it practically was. He'd approached her after a fashion show she had produced, a stunning art-meets-fashion affair held at the Getty during L.A. Fashion Week. She'd worked in fashion publicity for almost ten years after trying to be a celebrity publicist. She had been so nervous that her roommate convinced her to take a Xanax with a glass of chardonnay while she was getting ready. Hours later, after she'd careened between the models and fashion insiders backstage, he'd stopped her to introduce himself.

Cleveland wore a trendy but not-trying-too-hard blazer. He looked like he belonged backstage with those models. She should have been circulating, networking with the fashion industry bigwigs in attendance. But she couldn't break away. Cleveland made easy conversation, complimenting the show, the lighting and music, and even the vintage broach she'd thrown on at the last second, a lucky keepsake that belonged to her grandmother.

Candy looked over at her mother and sister, who looked out of place at the wedding, wearing clothes that didn't match the stylish, trendy wares of the other guests. Her mother sat there with a thin-lined frown. Candy's stomach tightened. Candy cut her eyes at her and back again. Her mother's lips twitched with silent words. Candy prayed that her mother would keep them to herself, though she had never really seen that happen, even as a child. Candy swallowed deep and hard. She knew her mother hated the thought of her marrying Cleveland after knowing him for a short time, and was maybe even a little jealous of his wealth and how he fawned over Candy. No one ever had fawned over her.

Candy had to admit that she and Cleveland had not known each other long. After just a few weeks of spectacular dates, she found herself sitting on Cleveland's smooth leather sofa in his living room, holding a glass of pinot noir from his favorite Napa vineyard, and looking out the floor-to-ceiling windows at his views of rolling hills and, if she squinted, the Hollywood sign.

She was contemplating how much a couch like this would cost when he said he needed to talk to her. She hated the sound of those ominous words, but he seemed energized and excited. So, how bad could it be?

That was the moment he would change her life forever.

After he was done speaking, she had sat there still and quiet, her mind blank with shock. He had just proposed marriage. A contracted marriage.

"I, Candy Miller Robertson, take you, Cleveland Rogers III, as my husband, to have and to hold…"

She looked out at their wedding guests, sitting in two rows. It was a large wedding with international guests, partners from Cleveland's law firm, and family. Her mother stood up on her feet in the middle of the vows. It was like the whole place held their breath. Candy darted a look as her mom quickly walked to the back and into the main house where the reception would be.

The vows started again. Heads focused back on Candy and Cleveland. But Candy couldn't think of nothing but her mother. She repeated the words in a robotic way.

At first, she chalked up her mother's disdain to the age difference —at twelve years her senior, he was nearing forty years old.

What Cleveland had proposed was more than marriage—or maybe less. He wanted a business arrangement, a contract to marry for five years. He described the mutual benefits for them both. He was on the verge of making partner at the top law firm in Los Angeles, with ties to the entertainment and finance worlds, and if he got married, the partners would welcome him more readily into their ranks. It didn't seem fair, he said, but every time they mentioned a social outing like the opera, or even a dinner party, the partners seemed embarrassed for him that he wasn't coupled up.

Cleveland was quick to offer all of the ways this would benefit her, too. She was twenty-eight years old, and after seven years in the fashion PR business, she hadn't gotten very far. She was working hard and taking orders from a demanding boss, while struggling to get recognition for her work. He would introduce her to fashion and entertainment bigwigs that would open so many doors for her. He would expose her to a life of luxury, extravagant dinners, weekends away in New York, Napa, or Hawaii. They would spend time together, support each other, learn from one another, but without the co-dependence and strangling intimacy he had struggled with in the past. When they walked into rooms together, Candy would be one of the few Black wives, if any. A rare chance to showcase the pride she had as a Black woman, her unique beauty and charm. She knew once someone reached a certain level, the issue wasn't just color any more but dollars and cents.

When Cleveland first laid the contracts on the desk, she'd been shocked. Twenty-three pages of legalese, paragraphs and subparagraphs, clauses, and little boxes for her initials. A cold sweat had crept down her back when she thought about the dangers of signing an agreement she couldn't understand to marry a man she hardly knew. But then she looked at him, his trusting eyes and eager smile, and she realized she did know him. More than that, she knew herself and what she stood to gain from taking such a big chance.

So, she read the twenty-three-page contract word by word over the next hour, stopping to ask the occasional question. Marriage of any kind was a risk, she realized. And whether or not she signed a contract or made promises in bed at night, it was still an agreement, two people each hoping the other would do what they said. In her case, she wanted to open up a world of luxury, travel, and business acumen, but for most it was a life of love, support, and partnership. It was always a risk, and she knew it was well worth the reward.

She picked up his heavy, monogrammed pen and signed her name on the last page where it asked for both parties' signatures. She stopped and looked up at him, at her future husband.

When they sat at their appointed long table at the reception, eating their foie gras and rib-eye steaks, drinking Moet, and laughing about Cleveland's latest drama at the firm, she wanted to feel like a gorgeous, privileged bride wearing a custom sheath wedding dress, showing off her glowing skin and ample cleavage. She looked down at the table at her mother and thought about all the clauses in the marriage contract she signed.

At that moment, Lettie stood up. It was time for the maid of honor's speech. Candy and the room listened as Lettie gave her sweet, doting words of admiration and respect for the happy couple. Next was the best man. It was the same congratulatory ramble—until Candy's mother clanked her glass loudly.

Candy looked away, at anything other than her mother, who knew the details of the contract. She prayed silently that she would keep her words brief.

"As the mother of the bride," Candy's mother cleared her throat. "I have to say that I am very pleased with her being in good hands with Cleveland and, uh, his way of life..."

Candy flashed a look at her mom. She held her glass so tight she thought she was going to break it. Cleveland squeezed her hand, almost like he sensed her nerves exploding inside her.

The room grew silent as Candy's mother searched for words. A few guests whispered to each other at the awkwardness.

"And, uh..." Candy's mom took a long sip from her glass and raised a finger. "I just want to say I'm an old-fashioned type, and I believe in real love. I would never be bought and sold. Who asks their wife to sign a—"

Candy launched up out of her seat and grabbed the mic from her mother.

Several guests gasped; a few others chuckled. Cleveland took her mother's hand and escorted her back to the table. She pushed him away several times as he walked her off, but he kept a firm grip until Lettie took over. It was obvious now how her mother felt.

"Maybe a few too many glasses, Mom?" Candy joked. The guests smiled with understanding eyes. Yet inside, Candy was horrified as she handed the mic back to the MC.

Lettie sat in horror, pleading with her sister to understand. But she just couldn't anymore. The most important day of her life her mom managed to ruin, once again.

1

Candy glanced at the passenger seat as she drove from the lawyer's office. Today marked her status as a single woman again. The divorce decree folder sat in an envelope, and just underneath that another folder had the old "Marriage Contract" written in red bold. As she waited in line to roll up to the restaurant valet, she scanned the old contract in her in mind. "Marital responsibilities," "work," "property in divorce," and "miscellaneous." She had put whatever she wanted on the miscellaneous pages of the marriage contract, mostly her monthly upkeep and extra allowances for hair, nails, makeup, clothes to keep it all together. These were typically transferred to her bank account on a monthly basis, including refills to her accounts at all the posh stores. She never used cash anywhere because everyone knew she was coming.

As she rolled up to the restaurant, she slipped the envelope in the glove compartment, away from the valet's prying eyes. She didn't want anyone to mess with it.

"Welcome, Ms. Robertson."

"Thank you," Candy said as she handed the keys to her white Range Rover to the young valet. "Please don't park it too far away."

Candy was meeting Elena, her friend of more than twenty years, for lunch at their favorite spot. Even though they had so much to catch up on, she had to stay on schedule today. In just two hours, she was due at the Fountain Day Spa for her facial with in-demand Misha, an appointment she'd made over three months ago for her post-divorce reset. Then she had a waxing appointment, followed by evening Pilates.

She relished her time with Elena. Candy had made peace with the fact that she couldn't have friends with the life she chose over ten years ago. Her lifestyle demanded privacy, discretion, and as few people involved as possible.

The two had met a few years after Elena's arrival from Romania, where she was born. They had met on a fashion set, where Elena did the makeup for the models. Candy mistook her for a model herself. Elena's dark hair, lean body, with high, sculpted cheekbones and light green eyes drew attention. She wasn't the most beautiful girl in the room, but she had an unusual look that Candy noticed right away, along with a low-key demeanor that Candy respected. They enjoyed partying together and even lived together for a short time as they both saved money. Three years after meeting, Elena married Michael, someone she had met in Romania, when he arrived in the States. Though their relationship changed, their bond didn't. Elena respected her boundaries as well as her time. Months would pass when they wouldn't speak, and they could still pick up the phone with ease. Elena was the only person who could tell her the truth, and Candy protected that ferociously.

Candy weaved her way through the tables of the crowded restaurant, smoothing her army green silk Philip Lim blouse. Elena bent over her phone, scrolling through Instagram. She always complained it sucked up too much of her time. Candy stayed off those platforms. She believed life's best was lived offstage, in the quiet, in the comfort of the secrets that she kept. This restaurant in particular, The Veranda, held a lot of secrets shared over lunch, too much wine, or the decadent chocolate cake. When she came here, she'd always seemed to notice someone in too deep conversation, even tears. She wondered why people went that deep in public, especially in such a gossipy town. She meandered through the white tables, alongside chatter and banter from hearts being mended and broken.

Finally, Elena greeted her with a wave. Her vibrant red lips looked like a painted-on target that couldn't be missed. She was sitting in their favorite back booth, next to a window overlooking the patio, a table that had hosted more of their private conversations over the years than Candy could remember.

"Sorry I'm late," Candy said, sliding into her seat. "I just came from the lawyer's office."

"I know how tedious lawyers can be. That's why we pay them the big bucks," Elena smiled. She looked cute as always, dressed in her usual sporty style. She had her long dark hair up in a ponytail, and a striped athletic-style top that could go from lunch to the yoga studio. Candy immediately caught the attention of the waiter, determined to make up for her lateness to her friend.

"I was beginning to wonder if you were coming," Elena said in her heavy Romanian accent. "I know today must be tough."

The waiter arrived tableside, lowering his head slightly to address them. "Excuse me, ladies, welcome. What can I get for you?"

"A bottle of the 2003 Château Laville Sauvignon Blanc, please," Candy said. The waiter nodded and headed off to retrieve the bottle. She looked at Elena. "I'm good, and we're celebrating. The papers are officially signed by Greg, and I'm free."

Elena made a face, skeptical at the idea of a celebration.

"It's just business, and Greg treated me very well," Candy countered.

"I know you say it's just business, but I still can't get over how you do these marriages," Elena said.

"All marriages are a business. It is a legal contract that affects each person's rights, including property. That's how it started back in the olden days. Ironically, if people used more business acumen, they'd be happier."

The waiter returned, pouring a generous amount of the wine into their glasses.

Elena smiled widely as she and Candace clinked their glasses together. They both took a long, quiet sip.

"I'm living proof that romantic feelings and love change," Elena said. "A marriage should be more than about love."

"Mutual respect and caring, shared interests, legal responsibilities, even healthcare," Candy said, recalling how in all the years of her mom's marriage she had none of those things except a man who claimed to love her. "And if he loves you, damn, that is icing on the cake. Love is a benefit of marriage, not the reason."

The waiter returned to take their order. Scallops for Elena and the lobster cobb salad for Candy.

"I never thought of it that way," Elena said, scratching her head, "but yes. It would clear up a lot of expectations early on."

Candy leaned in close. "Worldwide, eighty percent of people marry for many other reasons besides love. It's like Cleveland put it way back. *Everything in life is a deal. There's give and take, compromises and rewards, payment and services.*"

Elena nodded in agreement. "And look at all the charities you get to support. That would be a dream of mine. What about that charity Greg wanted to do?"

"I opened a basketball scholarship at his old Chicago high school in his name."

"I have to say your marriage to Greg was a good one. I'm sad to see it end. It was almost as good as Cleveland."

Candy took another sip of her wine. She never meant to fall in love with Cleveland, but it was her first of this kind of marriage.

"Things were less complicated with Greg," Candy said, perking up a bit. "He finally got the head coach gig he'd always dreamed of, thank you very much. I helped him focus, build trust with the heads of the league and the team owners, and navigate the delicate relationships with the wives. Remember, Greg was just a ball player who lucked out with the gig. And now he's making headlines as the first openly gay NBA coach. He looks good because he's being 'true to himself,'" Candy said with air quotes. "Even though that was the plan all along for his career. I look even better as the gracious wife who 'didn't know,'" Candy said, flicking her fingers up with air quotes.

The waiter came back with their food. They settled into their usual chitchat about their summer plans, their latest shopping trips, and some industry gossip.

"So, tell, me, you're happy with how things ended up?" Elena asked.

Candy dapped her mouth with the napkin. "Did I mention the beach house?"

"We had some good times there." Elena laughed. "And the views are gorgeous. Candy, that's a very nice *parting* gift."

"It is. He knows how much I loved that house, especially after I redid the downstairs for him last year," Candy said. The waiter returned and poured the chilled wine into their glasses, and took their finished plates away.

"I think he feels bad things got a little weird recently when he started dating Gabe. But I'm happy for him. I want him to be happy, and our agreement specified his other 'interests' from the beginning." Candy raised her glass. "To good friends, good wine, and life."

It always felt good to be herself with Elena. She could say anything and everything and not hold back. At moments like these, during an easy, comfortable exchange with someone she trusted implicitly, she felt the weight of most of her relationships. It took a lot of effort to be man's confidant and never let him in.

Midway through their meal, Elena looked up from her plate and asked, "So, I know you helped Greg fix his relationship with his mom. Are they still okay?"

"Yes," Candy said. "With her back in his life, he will be okay. I'm gonna miss that woman. Greg doesn't know how lucky he is." Candy paused, thinking about her mom and what they didn't have. They both finished their meals.

The sun was high in the sky, touching everything with the warm glow of spring. On the sidewalk, she saw a mother and daughter walk by holding hands. They stopped when the little girl pulled her hand away and seemed to ask to be picked up.

"Would you say the marriage was worth it?" Elena asked, breaking the quiet.

"The NBA is a whole different world than the Hollywood scene I know, so it's been a real education," Candy answered as the waiter cleared their plates. "But I'm done with athletes for now."

Elena laughed. "So, what's next? Or should I say, who's next?"

"Well, I haven't reviewed any potential clients yet," Candy said. "Truthfully, I needed a little time to myself."

"I've been married forever, and *I'd* like a break."

"I'm sure you do. But I bet after a night or two away, you'd be running home because you missed your man," Candy countered.

"You might be right about that," Elena agreed. "Any eager candidates lining up for their chance to be with Ms. Candy Miller Robertson?"

"In fact, there are," Candy said. "You'd be surprised how many men—or their publicists—reach out while I'm still married to see if I'm interested in grabbing dinner or a drink. And you know how secretive I am about what I do, so it's only word of mouth."

"Well, look at you. Aren't you just the hottest thing in town? How *ever* will you decide?"

They glanced at the dessert menus and knew what they wanted. Elena closed her menu with a flourish and waved over the waiter. "We'll have two cappuccinos and two cheesecakes."

After the waiter took their dessert menus and left, Candy turned to Elena. "I guess I'll be seeing you at Cycle House for the six o'clock class tomorrow."

"Take it easy. A little afternoon cheesecake never hurt anyone. Besides, you look like you can stand to gain a few pounds these days," Elena said, appraising her friend.

"I like to be at my best, married or not," Candy said, smiling.

"I suppose that means I should be looking for a bridesmaid dress soon?"

"Keep your calendar free."

"And what about the groom? What are you looking for this time?" Elena asked.

"It was fun with Greg, but we basically led two separate lives. I'd like a little excitement."

Then Elena stopped for a second and leaned in to Candy, "What if you fall in love?"

"Not—again."

2

Candy threw open the linen curtains, letting in the early morning sun. She watched the rough waves lap at the sand, mesmerized by the soothing rhythm. A waterfront property in Malibu would rent for quite a sum. Yet she almost couldn't bear the thought of someone else living here, sitting on her deck while taking in the sunsets or waking up in her custom king-size bed with the floor-to-ceiling ocean views. She'd spent hours painstakingly redecorating the house, choosing everything from the specific slabs of marble for the kitchen countertops to each piece of art and every throw pillow in the five bedrooms. It was modern and clean without being cold, a fine line that Candy worked hard to achieve. Plus, the light was incredible, filling her with such peace. This house was truly her refuge.

While she loved her lifestyle with her husband clients, she also longed for the autonomy of being alone. The obligations as a wife, including the roles and masks she had to wear in each relationship, were draining and exhilarating at the same time. She had to know when to push and when to step back and support.

She turned from the window and walked to the large, oval antique mirror over her dresser. She stopped to really look at herself.

She was getting older, and for the first time, she could feel it. She was almost forty, and while she took impeccable care of herself, often splurging on skin care, spa days, and a trainer, she could see the gentle tug of gravity, or perhaps exhaustion, that no amount of Pilates or laser treatments could fix. She touched her face, pulling and pushing, smiling and frowning. She had to admit, she was still beautiful. Her wide, almond-shaped eyes with long lashes were always her best feature. Her new, long haircut and perfectly placed highlights framed her face. These last few weeks of healthy eating, exercise, and more rest than she'd had in years helped. She was ready.

That evening—after a day filled with more maintenance, including a manicure, a spin class, and a stop at her favorite juice bar —the job of looking young and alluring was never finished. She was ready to open her files. She settled in at her desk with a glass of her favorite pinot noir and a stack of manila file folders.

Selecting her next husband would not be an easy process. She began by slowly sifting through an array of applicants. An influx of queries usually appeared after her divorce was announced, as if there was no time to waste. She asked for the same basic information before taking the process further. A letter of interest, professional details and goals, tax returns from the last five years, a list of properties and investments, and hobbies. The last one was more important than it seemed. How could she marry a guy who, to use a real example, preferred to spend his weekends flying to Rio for underground cage fighting? That wouldn't work for her, and it certainly wouldn't be a world where she could add value.

She opened the first file. Abraham Whitehead. Abe seemed interesting, though milder somehow, meeker than her other husbands. He was nearly twenty years her senior, and that seemed to match his pace. His hobbies included cycling and reading, both solitary pursuits. She imagined the quiet in his home, which might be good for this time in her life. But then again, didn't she do this for the excitement? And the age difference was too great for her to feel confident the relationship could provide any passion. She pushed his contract to the side.

No matter what, she wasn't going to settle. Not now, not at thirty-nine, with her rolodex and skill set. She could handle more adventure, more challenge.

On to the next. Xavier Oshun. Her lips curved in a smile at his name. He already sounded like a catch.

Xavier Oshun was thirty-five years old and gorgeous, six-foot-two with a slim build, a rugged jaw and neatly trimmed beard. He was an infamous Nigerian filmmaker, with deep dark, creamy skin and lush, curly hair. Worth millions, and now a Hollywood director living in L.A. He had never been married, no children, and his career was on the rise. His last film was the first in a huge A-list franchise, starring some of the biggest actors on the planet. The box office returns were astronomical, but he had reached a plateau.

Candy spent a few minutes scrolling through Google results. Finally, she began to see a pattern that might explain what he was looking for.

Headlines read, "Xavier Oshun cozies up to eighteen-year-old Victoria's Secret model," and "Affair! Oshun and married starlet Adha Audre caught in the act!" Not to mention the glaring red flag, "Director Xavier Oshun breaks down on set."

This would be a challenge, Candy laughed to herself. A reputation like that wasn't always accurate, of course. She knew how tabloids worked firsthand, since she'd been the subject of scrutiny right before Greg came out of the closet, while rumors were still swirling of his sexuality. People were rarely as interesting as they seemed in the news.

This could be promising. Xavier was a real Hollywood insider, with huge films on the docket and the kind of social circle she felt comfortable around. She knew she could help him smooth out whatever missteps he'd made in the past. She gazed again at his photo—the broad, easy smile and the warm brown eyes with a hint of mischief—and picked up the phone.

On the first ring, he answered.

"Mr. Oshun," Candy purred, sounding both sexy and self-assured. "This is Candy Robertson."

"Candy," he said genuinely. "I reached out a few weeks ago, and I wasn't sure if I was going to hear from you."

"Yes, well, I'm very in-demand, as you might know," Candy replied, already buzzing with flirtatious energy.

"I have no doubt," he said. "Can we meet soon to discuss an arrangement?"

"Certainly. But first I need a few questions answered," Candy replied. "What are your goals and intentions? What are you looking to accomplish?"

"I'm looking for companionship, someone who will put up with my crazy hours on set and, let's just call it, my difficult temperament. I'm tired of the game, of all of these wannabes and phonies who want what I have. I can't trust them."

"Why now?"

"I need to get to the next level. And I can't do it alone. I could use some help navigating the finer points of relationships with studio heads and producers. They do not understand my creative process. And their wives can be such bitches. I feel like the hired help some times." His passion, or perhaps anger, was seeping through. "I heard that you're quite good at winning people over and improving relations."

This was familiar. Candy nodded, hearing a tinge of his Nigerian accent. "You heard correctly. I can certainly help with your existing relationships, and perhaps help you to make some new ones. That all sounds reasonable."

Candy paused before asking, "And what about your personal life? Do you need help in that area?"

"Oh no, I've got my personal life all worked out," he said, laughing. "I focus on my work more than anything else."

Candy felt a light wave of disappointment. She didn't tolerate secrets and expected everything to be in the open. Her dignity was important to her. Even so, she knew from her research that his personal life consisted of a slew of young models and aspiring actresses that didn't stick around long. As long as he could concentrate on the task at hand, she could work with him. After all, it couldn't be harder than pretending to be the doting wife of a closeted NBA coach, could it?

"Children?"

"Not right now. And if we do this, you will get my family pushing us. Ignore them and just smile. I don't see me with kids for at least another ten years. Do you want children?"

"No," Candy said, firmly, but polite. She would never bring children into her lifestyle.

"Yes, of course."

"Xavier, I like what I'm hearing."

"So, dinner tomorrow?" he asked.

"Let's do it."

3

A tall, gallant man walked into the crowded restaurant with long, elegant strides, and Candy knew right away it was Xavier. He was dressed to kill in a navy Giuseppe Zanotti suit, unbuttoned at the neck with no tie. It was the perfect hybrid of too-cool-to-care and impeccably styled. The man knew how to dress, she'd give him that. He greeted the maître d' and made this way toward her table in the back. His presence reverberated around the room, causing other patrons to turn as he passed.

When Xavier had suggested they meet at the Cheron Timber, an exclusive French restaurant near the beach, she was surprised. It seemed like the kind of traditional, even stuffy, place that he would never go. The waiters wore tuxedos, and the décor was gold, ornate, some would say bordering on garish. She couldn't tell if he suggested the restaurant to appeal to her romantic side, or to show off, or if the choice revealed a deeper current within him.

Xavier arrived at the table, smiling warmly.

"It is such a pleasure to meet you, Ms. Robertson," he said, his large hand enclosing her own, a gentle yet firm caress.

"Hello, Xavier, call me Candy." She smiled, gesturing for him to sit. The waiter arrived to take their drink order, and Candy deferred to Xavier as he picked up the wine list, to see what he chose for himself or for them both.

"If you're a red wine drinker, I'd suggest a bottle of the Bonneau du Martray burgundy," he said confidently, closing the wine menu. "It's full bodied and quite sexy."

"Sounds apropos," Candy replied. A perfect choice for their first conversation. And she couldn't help but blush at his calling the wine sexy. *Not half as sexy as you are*, she thought. She could feel the spark of anticipation just below the surface. She couldn't deny that she was immediately attracted to him, and she leaned ever so slightly across the table. As good as he looked, she just couldn't help herself.

She was glad that she took the extra time to get ready before dinner. She was always put together, even for a quick afternoon of running errands. But tonight, she'd poured herself a glass of wine, painstakingly groomed her hair, and spent almost an hour on her makeup, creating understated smoky eyes. Plus, she was wearing her favorite killer black dress, the perfect tailoring of Elie Saab that made it sophisticated and elegant along with the plunging neckline that made her feel confident.

And now, sitting here across from a gorgeous, well-dressed, confident man, she was glad she did.

As the wine was poured, they fell into easy chatter, talking about the latest movie releases, their mutual friends in Hollywood, and even venturing onto his family. She had the sense that his parents coddled him growing up, and might still, and that he was used to getting his way.

Xavier was born and raised in an exclusive area of Lagos, the son of a big-time Nigerian businessman who had clearly pushed him to achieve greatness in whatever field he chose. She felt that familiar pang of jealousy whenever someone mentioned their parents taking an interest in their future, pushing them to go to college or to follow their dreams. She would have killed for that kind of support when she was younger. But she could see the pressure bothered Xavier. This tension seemed to be internalized, and he shifted quickly off the topic of his parents. He told her about going to NYU's film school and landing a lucrative contract with a major studio when he was just twenty-five.

Candy liked to play the role of the observer, listening as men told their stories. She watched how they smiled or laughed, or scowled, when they remembered certain moments or people. But it was what they didn't say that taught her the most about them.

She had a lot to learn about Xavier, and she still hadn't done a full background check yet.

After they ordered their meals, Candy asked, "How long do you want to be married for?"

"I'm not sure," he said. "What's the appropriate amount of time?"

"A year or so is good to start," she said. "That gives us enough time to be taken seriously and make some progress with your relationships in the industry. And it's probably longer than half the marriages in this town."

Xavier laughed and raised his glass. "I'll drink to that." After they toasted, he looked at her thoughtfully for a moment.

"What are you looking at?" Candy said, feeling his gaze. Unconsciously, her hand ran through her hair.

"You're beautiful, just *beautiful*. That's what I was thinking."

Emboldened by the compliment, she asked, "Are you surprised by that?"

"I'm not. But the truth is, this wasn't my idea. My agent and my publicist suggested I meet you and that working with you might be a way to improve my reputation. I've lost out a few jobs recently because these studio heads think I bring trouble wherever I go. It's such bullshit. My publicist thought you might be a good influence to help keep me out of trouble."

Candy smoothed out her napkin on her lap. "Why me?"

"It's important that I have a Black woman in my life. White women are always throwing themselves at me. But," he said, sitting back in his chair, becoming more thoughtful, "I grew up seeing Black couples in Nigeria doing powerful things together in business, and I want that. Make my family proud," he said, his eyes scanning her décolletage. "And, everybody wants you."

She looked up at him, searchingly.

He looked right back at her, holding eye contact and slid his hand over hers.

"But now that I'm sitting here across from you, looking at your beautiful, dark eyes, I just know this is supposed to happen. You and me."

It sounded like a line from a guy who had some success with lines. But she also sensed a genuine longing behind it, and at this particular moment, with the sexy French wine and the smile of a handsome man warming her body, she was willing to take it at face value.

After dinner—a decadent meal of beef bourguignon, creamy truffle potatoes, and more wine than she should have consumed—they walked out of the restaurant and into the crisp night. Candy felt a familiar sensation of hopefulness. *This is going to be great*, she thought. *He's gorgeous and exciting, and spending a year in his world would be the adventure I need.*

Candy looked at him as they waited. "Do you have any charity work or goals you want to do?"

He looked at her with a smirk. "No."

"We'll work on that." She smiled.

The valet pulled up in her car, and Xavier walked her to the door. "I'm really looking forward to this."

"Me, too," Candy said quietly.

Xavier leaned in for a hug. She liked his height, his warmth and sturdiness, and the feel of his arms around her.

"But let's not get ahead of ourselves just yet," she said as she pulled back, looking at him. "I need to run a background check first and then discuss terms with your attorney—*and* publicist."

"Of course, whatever you need." He smiled with the laid-back confidence of a man who always gets the girl. "So, what do you think after our first date? Do you like me?"

She always admired the assertive nature of a Nigerian man. "I only marry men I like."

Candy felt a wave of heat creeping up her neck. As much as she liked to keep it business, she enjoyed the attention from Xavier. It felt good to be desired. She tingled with the definite chemistry, albeit physical, and that was something she was longing for in a marriage, something she hadn't had since Cleveland.

She took a step toward her open car door and turned to say, "Well, Xavier. It's great to meet you. And I look forward to whatever comes next."

Smiling at her, he leaned in just enough that she thought he might kiss her. Her pulse quickened, and she couldn't breathe. Instead he said, in a soft tone, "Happily ever after."

4

———————

Candy woke up with the glow of a promising new beginning. Over dinner a few nights ago, Xavier had proved to be everything she had hoped for, and she'd spent a lot of time since then thinking about him. He was handsome and charming, successful and powerful—and a little damaged. She found his commitment to be seen with a Black woman endearing, and it would be even more important because their photos would be seen, and maybe even admired, by millions. She felt like she could help get his career to a new level, and she might enjoy herself doing it. She smiled as she remembered the buzz that rushed through her body when he leaned in, and she thought he might kiss her. The anticipation was almost better than the real thing. Almost.

Still, she had a long way to go before marrying Xavier, however much the thought of it made her smile. *Enough daydreaming,* Candy thought as she got out of bed and grabbed her robe.

She had a lot to do. First, she had to finish vetting Xavier and get the contract finalized. That included a trip to the law office today. Cleveland's law office. After their divorce, they had agreed that he would still look after her contractual affairs, albeit indirectly, with the help of one of his associates. She had secretly hoped that Cleveland would choose to do it himself, but she realized the awkwardness that would create. She wasn't willing to sacrifice getting the best legal advice from one of the best firms in Hollywood just because she no longer was married to the partner.

Candy entered her massive kitchen and fixed herself a frothy chai tea latte. She sat at the island, setting her white ceramic cup and laptop on the beautiful gray and white Carrara marble she'd hand-selected at a warehouse in Venice Beach. The hints of green amid the slight shimmer in the morning sunlight brought a smile to her face. As she drank her tea, she thought about what she was entering. She had to prepare herself to enter a new world of Hollywood's inner circle, on the arm of the rising star director Xavier Oshun. She'd need to do some shopping, of course, to revamp her look. She had been doing the youthful, athletic-leaning style of the NBA and the hip players' wives she was often entertaining. But now a more glamorous approach was more appropriate. It was time to gear up for battle.

She tidied up her kitchen, showered, and slipped into something businesslike yet casual. A navy-blue sheath dress that skimmed her body in the right places without being too tight or loose. She knew Cleveland would just happen to show up, as he always did. She didn't want him to get the wrong idea. Or at least, too much of the wrong idea. She slipped into a gray set of heels, dabbed on a fresh coat of lipstick, and in less than an hour, she was out the door.

As she drove to the law office, her mind started to wander to the time she met Cleveland. He'd known what he wanted and what he was capable of. He was way too focused on his career to enjoy real intimacy, and yet he needed a partner for events and to play hostess at dinner parties for his colleagues. She was young, struggling, clawing her way up for a measly two-percent raise each year. She wanted to know more about the world, meet the people that always seemed out of reach, and become the woman she'd always been meant to be. And, of course, get out of debt. She smiled to herself. She hadn't seen debt in years, and a bolt of gratefulness came over her. She nodded as she waited at the light.

She parked her car in the lot and walked into Cleveland's office building, her heart pounding in her stomach.

She checked in at the lawyer's office with the receptionist. Margie was a large-bodied, red-haired administrative "queen" of all office admins, which was how Cleveland described her twenty years of service. She knew Margie from her marriage to Cleveland, and Margie always kept it professional and friendly, never making her feel out of place. As she waited for Claude, the associate who would be helping her, she nursed a glass of prosecco, handed to her by the office hostess. Cleveland's office was a high-powered who's who, and everyone who was anyone came through the doors.

After a little while, Claude, a thirty-ish legal whiz in a brown tailored suit and suspenders, arrived. He was Cleveland's latest protégé and the third associate she had worked with in the last several years.

"My apologies, Ms. Robertson," he said, holding her hand, and apologizing again.

It had only been a ten-minute wait. "No worries, Claude. It's always a pleasure to see you. And I am always willing to wait for the best," she quipped, shaking his hand. "One of the best," she corrected. Their eyes smiled at each other, knowing exactly what she meant.

After several other niceties, they got down to business. They spent the next forty-five minutes discussing Xavier and the marriage. Claude asked her the usual questions. He reviewed the last contract with Greg, keeping most of what was in there. He also did an extensive search on Xavier's background.

"Mr. Oshun seems as clean as a crisp hundred-dollar bill. Everything checks out on this guy. Probably your most straight-laced prospect."

She took a long sip and sighed with relief.

Claude turned the screen with the results to face her so she could see. She squinted at the different entries, scanning to make sure she was reading everything right.

He had no public records, no lawsuits. He owned several properties along with domain names for them. She scrolled down for education and other details. However, she knew that the real dirt was never documented. It never appeared in a public record. She had learned the only way to really know was to live with a man. The results even contained his social media. She scrolled through his social media. Nothing. He barely had an IG account. It didn't surprise Candy. He was a director, not an actor, after all.

"Now the rest is up to me. I have to fine tune some of the details with his attorney," he said, writing down several notes.

"I know you have it handled, Claude. You always do."

"I learn from the best," he said, looking up, and pushing the papers aside.

"Speaking of—"

"He's good," Claude said, clearing his throat, and leaning in some. "He just came back from out of town."

Candy looked down at her shoes and up again. She didn't want to show her interest in why he had gone out of town. "Oh, is that right?"

"Yup," Claude said.

There was a brief silence.

"I'm sure he'd want to say hello before you leave."

Candy's shoulders relaxed. "I would like that."

Claude picked up the phone and called Cleveland's secretary.

"Thanks, Claude," she said, standing up. "This really gives me a peace of mind, knowing I have you, and this firm, looking after my affairs. Talk to you later?"

"Yes. I'll call you no later than tomorrow at noon with the final contract for your review. And I know Barry, his lawyer, and we should be good on this. You'll be taken care of."

Claude walked Candy down the long hall way to Cleveland's brooding corner office. The walk seemed to take forever. She hadn't seen him in a while.

They opened the door, but Cleveland wasn't there.

"He may have just stepped away for a few minutes. Wait here. Good to see you again," Claude said and walked back down the hall.

Candy got comfortable in one of the chairs as she waited. Her mind wandered to what Claude had said about learning from the best. Cleveland had also taught her well. Sometimes, when he was in the middle of a big case, he would call her into his study and talk through both sides of the argument until ultimately, he'd land on his clinching point, the sure way to win. And while Candy often only listened during this exercise, she learned more than most third-year law students on how to negotiate successfully and never back down from a fight.

Watching Cleveland conduct business, particularly after he made partner and settled into the role with more confidence and entitlement, taught her valuable lessons on how to get what she wanted. He would build a rapport, go in softly talking of partnerships and the importance of a mutually beneficial relationship, until the final push was needed. And then it was as if disagreeing with him was not a business decision but a personal affront.

Candy applied this technique to so much in her life, particularly when she was discussing the terms of her contracts. What she also had working in her favor was being one of only few Black professional wives in a business dominated by white women. Scarcity upped her value.

"Ms. Robertson." She turned around at the female voice. It was Marge.

"Mr. Cleveland said he will arrive in the next ten minutes. He's walking over. Do you need anything?"

"I thought he was here already."

Margie blushed. "He wanted to be notified before you left. So, he is on his way back from a lunch. He didn't want to miss you."

"Oh," Candy said, feeling flattered.

"Are you in a rush?"

"Not at all, Margie."

Margie nodded and left. Candy knew that Cleveland probably was racing across town in his chauffeured Town Car to meet her. If she had known he was not here, she would not have waited. He did know her well.

She settled back into the comfortable chair. The deal with her next husband was done, and she felt exultant as she always did. That very afternoon, on her way to pick Elena up for a day of shopping, she would stop by the law office to sign the hard copies of the agreement. In the next few days, she would be wired her signing payment, a cool $7.5 million dollars, with the other half due on completion of the year.

As she sat in Cleveland's office, so familiar from years past, her mind wandered. Soon her thoughts roamed all the way back to their beginning. On their first date, they went to a sushi restaurant, where instead of ordering off the menu, the chef brought them his specialties over twelve courses. She was nervous, because normally she wasn't that adventurous, choosing a simple California roll or maybe spicy tuna. But she'd let Cleveland's sophisticated manner infect her, and before she knew it, she was giggling over the feel of fish roe bursting in her mouth and savoring the pièce de résistance, sea urchin.

All the different flavors collided on her palate, pushing her out of her comfort zone. Just like their first kiss later that night as he dropped her off at the door of her West Hollywood apartment building, his black Town Car idling in front conspicuously.

Their next few dates flew by in similar fashion. At a Lakers game, she sat so close to the court, she was worried the players would run into her, followed by another incredible dinner, this time on the water in Santa Monica, where they watched the sun set.

She was happily remembering how Cleveland held her tight when suddenly he walked through the door, a few drops of sweat on his forehead.

She bolted upright and snapped off a quick joke. "I don't want you to give yourself a heart attack."

They both laughed as he dabbed his forehead with a handkerchief. "It's too late for that, remember?"

They laughed some more as they hugged, warmly, just short of lingering.

Cleveland sat down behind his desk and gleamed at Candy. "You are stunning. As always. Thank you for waiting for me."

She felt so at ease with him. "It's been a minute, Cleveland."

"I know. I'm just glad to see you're okay."

"I am," she said. "The divorce was quick, thanks to Claude's iron-clad agreements."

"And this new person?"

"Xavier Ohsun."

"Is this one gay, too?"

"He's not. He seems like a regular guy."

Cleveland smirked. "In Hollywood? Nothing is regular."

"How's bachelorhood treating you?"

Cleveland's mouth formed a thin line, and he sat back abruptly in his chair "Uhm, it's okay. I mean, it depends. What I mean is—"

Candy's mouth flew open. "Not *you* at a loss for words?"

He looked away from her, glancing at his computer screen.

She took the hint. "Okay, well, I guess I will go and let you get back to work."

He seemed to catch himself. With his usual casual grace, he walked her to the door. "Until next time," he said, half-shaking, half-caressing her hand.

She let go first and left. As she came out of the building, she couldn't shake the feeling that something had changed.

When she got back in her car, her phone rang. She picked it up quickly, not seeing that she almost went through a red light. She was pleasantly surprised to hear Xavier's baritone voice on the other end.

"Am I in?" he asked.

"Why wouldn't you be?" Candy asked, zipping on the highway on the way to meet Elena.

"Well, you didn't return my calls, so—"

"I wanted to handle the business at hand before we spoke again. But now that's settled, I'm glad to hear from you. Your lawyer should be talking to my lawyer now."

"They are." Xavier laughed. "My lawyer just emailed me everything."

Candy noted the lightness in his tone. *Could he be nervous?* she wondered.

"How are you?" he asked.

"I'm good. Heading out shortly for a day of shopping with a friend. I want to make sure I'm prepared for all of the events and parties we'll be going to," Candy said. "I'm sure your social calendar is quite full." Candy knew this deal was sealed by the tone of his voice, and she had to seal it; she wanted Xavier.

"I like the sound of that, walking into a party with the most beautiful woman in the room on my arm."

Candy smiled at the thought of being on Xavier's arm and couldn't get out any words for a moment. *Oh no*, she thought, *keep it together*.

"So, the next steps. Sign the contract. We should then be seen together in the next few days and get some paparazzi shots taken. Then we can announce the engagement in a few weeks. I'd suggest a destination wedding, maybe a dozen friends on the beach, so we can do it quickly. Sound good?" Candy brought the professional edge back to her voice.

"Of course, yes. That all sounds good. Looking for my pen now."

"I also need to meet your publicist."

"Sure. I can arrange that," he said. "Can I see you tonight? Can we celebrate?"

"Sure, we can. Tell your publicist we'll be at LaLu at eight o'clock," Candy said matter-of-factly. "Have them call a few photographers to catch us walking in and out. By tomorrow, we'll be an official couple."

5

———————

By the time Candy picked up Elena and headed to their favorite shops, she was already exhausted. The girls planned a dual approach. Hit the designer mecca of Rodeo Drive and then mix it up with some of their vintage favorites to get those one-of-a-kind conversation pieces that turned their style from designer showroom impressive to truly inspired.

Candy focused on updating her basics, well-tailored, beautifully cut cocktail and day dresses, blazers and blouses paired with perfectly fitted dark denim, and shoes that added a hint of interest. From Max Mara to Saint Laurent, Ferragamo to Miu Miu, and even a stop at La Perla—Candy and Elena pursued the racks slowly, enjoying the afternoon together and contemplating all of the fun, star-studded evenings when Candy would wear her new items.

Elena examined every piece she tried on and gave her the kind of honest feedback Candy could only get from her lifelong friend. "Too short" or "too long," "too matronly" or "too slutty." Elena critiqued everything until Candy emerged with only a handful of items, and they were perfect.

Elena's willingness to give tough-love feedback on the clothes reminded Candy of Cleveland. When they first met, she was wearing hand-me-down pieces from her colleagues at the fashion PR firm and leftovers from photo shoots. She couldn't afford to buy anything nice of her own, and she knew she would be ridiculed if she showed up to work wearing H&M's finest. But the result was a hodgepodge of mostly ill-fitting runway castoffs from past seasons.

Early on in their relationship, Cleveland knew he had to help her. Besides wanting a presentable, well-heeled wife on his arm, he wanted to help her grow up and take control of her look and her life. And he really did know what stores she should be shopping in and what pieces flattered her shape. He was patient but insistent. Ultimately, he helped her create a sense of style that had endured for the last fifteen years.

As she shopped, fragments of her conversation with Cleveland in his office, lingered in her mind. What was he trying to hide? The way his mood shifted at the end of their meeting. Maybe he just didn't want to admit he was having trouble meeting the right person. No one ever really wanted to talk about that. Though she felt that in their relationship, at least what it used to be, they could talk about anything.

She and Elena loaded her packages into the trunk of her Range Rover and began the drive back to Candy's house in Malibu for an evening of sharing a bottle of champagne and getting Candy ready for her date. She'd spent a small fortune on clothes, sure, but more than that she felt prepared to begin this next chapter. She had the right pieces to create a new persona, the slightly different version of herself that would thrive with Xavier under the bright lights of the Hollywood scene.

She smiled, knowing Cleveland would approve of her shrewd negotiating skills and her innate sense of style. When she really stopped to think about all that Cleveland had taught her, she was astonished. And so grateful.

Taking him up on his unusual proposal was the bravest thing she'd ever done.

~

"It's me," Candy heard the soft, quiet voice say on the other end of the line.

"You okay?" Candy said as she started to wind down for the evening.

"Can you stop by tonight? We have a problem."

Those words were not music to Candy's ear. "What's up, hon?"

"Mommy hasn't paid the mortgage. We are like months behind. I just found out when I went through the mail today. The lights are out, too."

Candy sighed. "Is she home?"

"No."

"I'm on my way." Candy pulled on a pair of sweats and hopped back in her car. It seemed that she had been doing nothing but driving lately.

Within fifteen minutes, she was at her childhood home. Lettie opened the door, wrapping her arms around Candy.

Candy hugged her sister tightly, inhaling her sweet Jasmine scented hair. Lettie, standing at five-ten, was just a few inches taller than Candy, with cropped hair and a long, athletic body. Candy was proud of the woman her twenty-year-old sister was becoming.

Lettie led Candy into the darkened house.

"Don't worry, she's not back yet. Her shift at the bar ends at midnight."

Candy looked around and realized nothing really changed. There were unopened boxes and old clothes and dirty plates strewn everywhere. She had thought her mother would use the money she sent to make the house look good. It was the first house Candy could afford to buy them. What, exactly, was her mother doing with the money?

Candy caught up with Lettie about school and work. Lettie had dashing hazel eyes set against her dark skin. Her hair, mixed with her father's Indian ancestry, flowed down her back. Candy thought her sister was the most beautiful woman in the world. She just needed Lettie to believe that, too.

"Here you go," Candy said, giving her a stack of hundred-dollar bills. She never gave checks or made money transfers to her mom's bank account. Her mother received public assistance, and told her anything like that would mess up her benefits.

Lettie counted the money, and her eyes flew open. "Ten thousand dollars?"

"Take out what you need for yourself, and use the rest for the bills."

Lettie nodded. "I'm sorry that every time you come here, it's about money. What would we do without you?"

Candy sighed.

"I can drop out of school and work more—"

"No," Candy said, putting her hand on her sister's. "Finish school. Please."

An odd sight out the window caught her attention. "Who does that BMW belong to?"

"Mommy."

Candy nodded. That's where the money was going. "What do you drive?"

"I have that same Honda from years ago. I use my money for school."

"And you're saving the money I send to you?"

"I try, but if something needs to get done around here, she'll give me some sob story. I just give it to her, or I won't hear the end of it. I really can't have anything without her wanting it, too."

Candy nodded. "She's up to the same things. She thinks you having money will empower you to leave her. She's using it so you can't."

Tears began to stream down Lettie's face. "I know she needs me, but whatever I do is not enough. Living around here is expensive, and I don't want to move far."

"You can stay with me," Candy said, not thinking twice about it.

"No," Lettie waved frantically. "I want to be able take care of myself like you do. And you live too far from my school."

"Mommy is fine. She's lived her life. What about you?"

Lettie wiped her tears.

"Lettie, you gotta start planning for your own future."

Lettie nodded again. "I'm not a school person. I like working. I like making money."

Candy felt bad for pushing her sister, but they rarely got to see each other. She rubbed Lettie's back. "Let me cover school for you. I know working and paying for school is hard. And I can get someone to work on a few investments for you."

"Let me think about it." Lettie smiled.

"Are you seeing anyone?"

"I met a nice guy at school. But he lives on campus, and we don't see each other a lot. So, I don't know." She rolled her eyes.

As she talked to Lettie, it struck Candy how far she had come. From the squat yellow ranch she grew up in to living in mega mansions. Her childhood home had three bedrooms and two bathrooms, so it wasn't tiny by any means. But when she, her sister, and her parents all lived there, it seemed to shrink from the weight of their drama. She thought of her father slamming the chipped front door after another late night, his heavy footsteps shaking the floorboards as he lumbered down the hall. She shuddered. She hadn't thought of him in a while, and she wouldn't start now.

She was a sophomore in high school when he finally left for good, and she'd expected their family life to improve considerably. But that wasn't the case. Only after he was gone did the extent of the debt he'd racked up in her mother's name come to light. Bill after bill was delivered in the mail, and creditors began calling her mom. When she went to the bank to get the mess all sorted out, she realized that he'd taken a second mortgage on the house and ran off with thirty-grand. They never saw him again.

After taken care of things for Lettie, Candy relaxed. They said their goodbyes, and she went back home.

The next morning, she got a text with an image of a paid mortgage statement and electric bill.

Candy smiled at it. She admired how organized Lettie was and prayed she'd get out on her own soon. A small part of her hoped she'd hear from her mother. Her mother knew where the money came from. But Candy never felt acknowledged as a child or even now.

At least with this latest drama put to bed, she could start "dating" Xavier with a clean slate.

6

The following week, Candy and Xavier were the new "it" couple in town. Photos of their dinner at LaLu had spread fast, and tabloids were rushing out any information they could find on their relationship. Xavier's publicist planted a few seeds with trusted reporters, so their backstory was beginning to develop in the public eye.

They'd been old friends who reconnected at an Oscars party. Xavier is happier than ever.

The spin was immediately positive, with headlines claiming "playboy director" Xavier Oshun had finally settled down.

Xavier's team couldn't have been happier with the response in the media and within the executive suites of Hollywood. They were pushing Xavier and Candy to host an intimate dinner party soon, inviting studio bigwigs and talent from his next film.

"So, what do you think?" Xavier asked Candy.

"I want to wait until I am fully settled and moved in."

"It only seems fitting that we live together first when we announce our engagement." He smiled, hugging her by the waist.

The move took only an afternoon with a small team of white-glove movers packing her wardrobe and a few key pieces of furniture, leaving the majority of furniture in the Malibu house. A European couple looking to spend six months in Los Angeles was paying almost ten thousand dollars a month to live there.

Xavier left for the afternoon, while Candy directed the house help on what to do with her things. Xavier's housekeeper Greta was on hand to welcome Candy.

"Ms. Robertson, I have it all handled. You just tell me what you need," Greta said. Her grandma-natured tone helped to ease Candy's mind.

"Thank you, Greta. I haven't the slightest idea where anything belongs. This home is amazingly huge," Candy said, looking above at the cathedral ceilings.

"Oh, I can sure help you around," Greta said.

"Don't worry, I'm okay. There's already a lot to do." Candy didn't want to distract Greta from the main object at task. Getting her things moved in.

Greta directed the movers to the large closet in one of the upstairs bedrooms that Candy would make her dressing room. While they brought in her belongings, she took the opportunity to walk around and check out her new home herself.

The house was traditional, built in the late fifties with six bedrooms and six bathrooms. Though not quite her style, it was beautifully appointed in a masculine yet approachable way. There was a lot of brown and camel leather furniture, deep navy throw pillows and light, creamy walls. One of her favorite rooms was a large den/office combination with a heavy oak desk on one end and a seating area with the softest, most inviting sofas in butterscotch leather. She opened a few of the desk drawers and rummaged around, unsure of what she was looking for.

Candy entered the master suite, a grand room with a reading nook by the window, a large walk-in closet, and views of the terrace and pool, with the Hollywood hills rising behind. *I could get used to waking up here*, she thought as she ran her hand over a dresser, fingering a few photographs, knickknacks, and a stack of books. She paused in front of the mirror. She ran a finger across the natural arch of her thick eyebrows, then turned her face side to side to check her makeup. She adjusted her long-sleeve tunic over her hips, relishing the *clink-clank* of her stack of delicate gold bangles. She could grow to like the new look she was taking on.

After the movers left, she went to her dressing room to get organized. This would be her command center, the one place in Xavier's home she could call her own. She inspected her clothes, hanging in the well-lit, freshly painted closet, and began organizing them by color. She then turned her attention to her vanity with its upholstered baby blue velvet high-back chair that she'd brought from home. It made her feel so glamorous when she got ready, and it was going to be a year of feeling glamorous, so why not bring it?

As she put the finishing touches on organizing her accessories and ample shoe collection, she was alerted by a knock at the door. Xavier stood in the doorway, holding two dozen pink peonies and a bottle of champagne.

"I'm so sorry I had to leave earlier," he said. He took a few steps across the room, presenting the flowers. "These are for you. I hope you like peonies. I can have Greta bring you a vase."

"Thank you! These are beautiful," she said, inhaling the fragrant aroma.

"Wow, you've really settled in," he said as he took in the tidy shelves, cosmetics lined up neatly in a row, and the full closet.

Candy blushed and said, "Yes, well, I thought it better to get organized."

"I love it. I want you to be happy," he said quickly. "Let's toast. Come outside and we'll watch the sun set."

Candy raised her glass, taking a long, slow sip of the champagne. She let the bubbles burst on her tongue and the late afternoon sun warm her face. Greta had put out an array of artisanal cheese and crackers, a platter of fruit, and an array of nuts. If Candy wasn't careful, she could gain twenty pounds just breathing the air in. Everything felt sumptuous.

Xavier leaned back in his chair, his oversize sunglasses hiding his eyes. He was furiously typing on his iPhone and moving his lips a little. He grew more and more agitated, until he slammed his phone down on the table and polished off his glass.

"Everything OK?" Candy asked.

"I have to re-pitch a project I already sold to the studio. There's a new head of development in place, and apparently, he doesn't have the basic sense of the last one, so I have to go in there and sell him on it. What I really want to do is throw him through a window for making me jump through these hoops. Doesn't he know who I am? Haven't I had enough box office wins to get a green light without bending over?"

"You can always view it as an opportunity to make a new connection. You can establish an even better relationship with him than the last guy," Candy said, hoping she wouldn't hit a nerve.

He eyed her for a moment, silent and expressionless. Candy held her breath, hoping it wasn't too soon to give advice. Men were delicate that way. You had to warm them up and earn their trust before doling out advice. Just when Candy thought she'd moved too quickly, Xavier broke into a wide smile and poured them both more champagne.

"I suppose I could." He chuckled. "Now, why didn't I think of that?"

"In fact, your publicist mentioned having that dinner party soon. Why don't you invite him?"

He reached across the table and squeezed her forearm affectionately. She felt a jolt as his fingers and then his palm touched her skin.

"That's a great idea," he said. "Look at you, here for five minutes and already talking me off the ledge. Now, when can I marry you?" He winked as he took another sip of champagne and looked at her expectantly.

"Well, let's see. We've officially been a couple for two weeks, so I think another week or two will do it. Maybe we can announce it at our dinner party."

"And I imagine we'll need a ring to make it official, won't we?"

"Yes, I think that's customary," Candy said.

"What would a beautiful woman like you want on her finger? A simple cushion cut solitaire, an antique setting with a story... Or doesn't it matter as long as it's big?" He teased.

"I - trust -you," Candy said, lingering on every word.

7

———————

Candy began her first morning living with Xavier the same way she began most mornings. She woke early, wrapped her long silk robe around her, and made her way to the kitchen for something hot. She and Xavier decided to ease their way into the relationship, so he slept in another bedroom. She appreciated the gesture, but she had to admit she was a little disappointed that their night of sipping champagne and talking about rings hadn't turned into more. He was up and out early this morning, first meeting with his trainer for a boxing session, which explained the firm, chiseled look under his T-shirt, and then working with the editors to put finishing touches on his film coming out that summer. She'd have the day to herself, which meant she could relax and get acclimated, and maybe even have Elena over to check out the house.

Candy sat at the kitchen table banquet while Greta brought her a cappuccino and a grapefruit. She had to admit that she could get used to this. In between sips of the creamy brew and looking out at the morning sun glinting off the surrounding hills, Candy flipped through a few newspapers and magazines from the pile on the counter.

When she opened her phone, she froze. Cleveland popped up in her newsfeed. In the photo he was walking with a beautiful woman, holding hands and smiling. Candy's heart dipped. *Cleveland.* The short caption said, "Daytime Diva Marlene Gavinci has a new man!"

Marlene Gavinci was a well-known talk show host, with a big mouth and even bigger personality. Her show was a combination of gossip and celebrity news followed by superficial interviews with B-list celebrities hawking their latest projects. She wasn't a serious journalist, of course, but she had a certain amount of cultural cache because she was photographed often on red carpets and on the arm of gorgeous men around town. She was the type of celebrity Candy saw regularly without ever really registering who she was. And now she was smiling ear to ear at Cleveland—*her* Cleveland—as she strutted down Melrose in four-inch espadrilles.

Was this what Cleveland was hiding?

Candy shouldn't let this news bother her. Of course, she shouldn't. It was absurd. She was about to be married to one of the most eligible bachelors on Hollywood's A-list, living in his ten-million-dollar Hidden Hills home, sipping a cappuccino made by her new housekeeper. *She* was living the life! So, what if Cleveland wanted to run around with some casual fling while the paps took his photo. He probably regarded Marlene as a novelty, like elderflower liqueur in your cocktail—new and interesting on the palette, but not life changing.

Unless of course, it was.

Candy broke into a cold sweat when she thought about Cleveland and Marlene Gavinci getting serious. She had to know more. She left the table in the sunny corner of the kitchen and practically ran to her dressing room to get her laptop. Lying on her daybed, she began searching for everything she could find on the new couple. There wasn't a lot. They'd been photographed together only once before, one of those grainy long-lens photos of them canoodling in a booth at the back of a dimly lit restaurant. Hardly a marriage proposal, but she had to admit that they looked smitten.

Her phone buzzed, startling her. Elena would be there in twenty minutes, which meant Candy needed to get dressed and stop this nonsense. Besides, Elena would arrive just in time to watch Marlene's show at eleven.

The doorbell rang just as Candy slid on her Jimmy Choo gold strappy sandals. Candy walked to the top of the stairs to see Greta opening the door wide for Elena, who looked immediately impressed.

"Hey, lady!" Candy said, waving her in.

Elena greeted her back, thanked Greta, and marched up the steps before Candy could go down.

They hugged and Candy took Elena around.

"This isn't bad," Elena said, grinning.

"I think I'll manage here for a while," Candy said.

They both laughed. Candy gave Elena a tour, first of her dressing room, then a few of the other guest rooms, and finally the master with its incredible views. Then they headed downstairs to the media room/den, where they sat on a peacock blue, deep tweed couch.

"Well, I've been married for ten years, and I can't even get Michael to repaint the downstairs." Elena looked around, touching the delicate fabrics of the curtain, the mahogany desks, and marble fixtures. "And you have all this instantly."

Candy smiled. She didn't want to rub her new life in Elena's face, but it did feel good. "Honey, you know what I go through to do this. You've got the real thing. This is all make-believe, just like most things in Hollywood."

"I know, I know. I'm not complaining. I'd just like a little magic in my life these days, that's all," Elena said.

Candy felt badly for Elena. Real marriage was tough, and the ten years with Michael hadn't always been easy. She knew that Elena's marriage had been in trouble in the last year or two.

Candy picked up the remote and flipped to the right channel.

Elena groaned. "Oh geez. Is there a reason we're watching *that* garbage?"

"There sure is…" Candy said, settling back in the oversize throw pillows. "You'll see soon enough."

Marlene's bright, Easter-colored set filled the screen. The stage was periwinkle, with a faux stained-glass panel in various pastel shades behind it. Two beige armchairs stood in the center behind a low modern coffee table with two mugs and an arrangement of roses. The audience applauded, hooting and hollering as the music turned up, and Marlene strutted out from behind the center panel. She waved to her audience and the cameras, danced a little, and stopped and took a small bow before taking her seat and looking into the camera.

"Goooooood morning, y'all!" Marlene bellowed. "I'm just so glad we're all here together, discussing the latest and greatest in pop culture news. And boy, there is sure a lot to keep up with these days! I mean, someone posted a selfie on Instagram with her new ballplayer boy-toy before deleting it only minutes later. What could that mean? And which Hollywood royalty couple may not be calling it quits, after all? So much to discuss! But first, there's a little something in my own life that I want to share with you. I mean we're friends, aren't we?"

The audience went crazy, screaming and applauding. Candy turned to Elena and said, "This is it."

"I am pleased to tell you that I have a special new man in my life. Yes, that's right, I'm one happy lady these days. And I have even better news to share. He proposed!" Marlene held up her hand, showing off a large, shimmering diamond engagement ring to viewers. The camera panned in. Candy's mouth went dry.

"The lucky man I'm going to marry is a well-known mega attorney here in Los Angeles. I know, I know—who wants to marry a lawyer? But believe me, he's not boring!"

The crowd went wild again with hoots and hollers.

"He's fabulous, and we've had so much fun together over the last few months. Here are a few pictures of our latest exploits...."

Photos filled the screen. First, Cleveland and Marlene sitting in a café in Paris, toasting with glasses of red wine, the Eiffel Tower visible in the distance. Another of Cleveland and Marlene at a street market in Dubai. She looked happy and windblown, a billowing creamy scarf around her neck. And, Candy hated to admit to herself, he looked like he was in love. The last photo was taken from the ground as a hot air balloon was coming in for a landing. Marlene was smiling wide and had her hand in the air, showing the photographer her new jewelry. Cleveland was standing behind her, arms wrapped around her tightly, face buried in her neck.

"Oh my God," Elena said, stunned.

Candy could feel Elena's eyes on her, but as long as the photos were on the screen, she couldn't turn away from the TV to look at her.

"Are you OK?" Elena asked tentatively. "I mean, I know things ended pretty well with him, and you never said anything differently, but I always had the feeling there was something more. That maybe you had feelings for him ... What are you thinking?"

Candy couldn't articulate what was going through her mind. No matter how strongly she felt about Cleveland while they were married, it was a business arrangement. She could never compete with a woman that he proposed to in a hot air balloon. She thought he couldn't do intimacy or serious. That's why he made the proposal to her in the first place. But apparently, he could do intimacy. Just not with her.

"I'm fine, really," Candy said, putting on a smile and turning to Elena. "I thought I heard something about him settling down, and I thought it would be funny to watch together." She focused on taking calm, even breaths.

Elena was about to say something when she heard a man's voice by the front door.

"My wife-to-be," Xavier said as he sauntered into the den, taking off his leather jacket. "And hello, Candy's friend."

"Xavier, this is Elena, my best friend. She's been with me through everything," Candy said, winking at Elena, who studied Xavier from head to toe.

"It's wonderful to meet you, Elena," Xavier said, smiling. "I don't mean to interrupt you. I'm home early after problems at the editing suites, so I'm going to make some calls. You two go back to whatever you were doing."

"Nice to meet you, Xavier," Elena said.

Xavier left the room as coolly as he entered, and Elena turned to Candy.

"Wow," Elena said, watching him walk out. "He's not bad to look at."

"No, he's certainly not," Candy said, looking down the hall at him.

Reluctantly, her gaze returned to the TV. Marlene held her ring finger to the camera again, proud to show it off to all the world. Candy winced, biting back the pain that threatened to spill.

8

———————

arlene. Candy said to herself, still in disbelief. Sitting alone in her private bathroom, she looked at her reflection and frowned at herself for carrying poisonous thoughts of Marlene in her head all night. She reasoned that Cleveland must be under some influence to marry such a woman. But then again, he married her years ago, too, and she wasn't exactly the Virgin Mary.

Annoyance grew inside her at Cleveland for hiding such news from her. On impulse, she picked up her phone to call him. "Hello, Marge. Cleveland, please."

"Sure, Candy, one second."

Within a few seconds, Marge returned and said, "He's unavailable now."

"As in out of the office?"

Marge paused. "Yes."

Candy hung up and drew in a deep breath. Marge was lying, she thought, and that was okay. She refused to wallow in anything less than what she deserved.

She had no sooner put down her cell phone when it beeped.

"Can't wait to get back home to you this afternoon," texted Xavier.

Candy typed a heart emoji and clicked "Send."

After less than a week of living together, Candy thought that Xavier was right on course. He courted her like she was a normal woman, which she missed. She slipped into white skirt and slid on a white and navy-striped tube top. With her hair pulled up, her usual confidence shined on a day she was feeling other than blissful.

The afternoon with Xavier, she hoped, would be exactly what she needed to regain her focus.

The clatter of voices downstairs signaled to her that Xavier was home. He always walked in with something to say to the help. A bit of mild chatter, a light laugh.

Xavier called out loud and clear, "Babe, you ready? Taking you out on the boat this afternoon." He held a bouquet of red roses. "Surprise."

"Those are beautiful." Candy peeked over the banister. "I'm ready whenever you are." She walked down the steps, taking each step in stride.

She fell into his arms and inhaled the clean scent of the roses. She gave them to Greta and laid her head on his shoulders. "Mmm, I feel good in your arms."

"You mean that," he said, gazing at her.

"I do." She grabbed his hand, along with her bag.

From a small digital pad at the door, he summoned the car to meet them in the front.

The ride to the boat was quiet. Candy liked that they could sit in silence. She felt a natural comfort level with him. She felt like Xavier was a good guy who just needed help, her help.

"How are you liking it so far?" he asked, looking over at her with a glass of champagne in his hand.

"Everything is good, and I have a feeling it's going to get better," she said, taking a sip from her flute.

A large white yacht emerged as they arrived at Marina Del Rey. The driver turned the corner as gentle rising waves filled the background.

Xavier exited the car and opened her door. He extended his hand

and helped her onto an imposing fifty-foot yacht. An attractive older gentleman in a captain's hat and uniform waved to them as they walked up.

"This is breathtaking, Xavier," Candy said, her hand over her mouth.

"Coming from you, that means a lot. I know you've had the best."

"I have, certainly," she said, unashamed. "Did you call the press?"

"All done, and it will be discreet," he said as they climbed the steps to the boat. He escorted her to a bench on the deck. A nearby table had a chilled unopened bottle of wine and a delectable spread of seafood, fresh greens, meats, breads, and condiments. She looked at Xavier for an explanation for the extravagant display. She was almost sure more people had to be invited.

He took her hand without saying a word and led her to the bow. A white, fluffy lounging sofa with a gray, lush blanket and cushions and a bottle of chilled champagne next to another platter of fruit and nuts awaited them.

"Is this all for us?" Candy couldn't help herself.

"Yeah, I figured, get as much as we need or don't need. Wasn't sure what you liked. Besides, who knows how long we'll stay on here? We may get stranded out at sea."

Candy liked his foresight and chuckled.

He took a deep breath, nuzzled his nose around the nape of her neck. She relaxed in his arms, feeling his hardness growing behind her.

For a business arrangement, this was above and beyond, she thought. She really expected a more direct approach, to the point. They had plenty of time for fanfare, she thought. But inside, she loved it. The yacht navigated out of the marina, and soon they were out on the open sea. Xavier turned to her, looking dashing in white linen pants and shirt, broad, square shoulders, trimmed beard, and a fierce, longing gaze that locked onto her. He took her hand.

"Candy, will you marry me?" he asked with the same intense look in his eye.

A feeling came over her when she looked at him. It felt real. She wanted desperately for it to be real. And she silently thanked him for making it feel that way. "Yes. I will."

Xavier smiled and slid a beautiful seven-carat cushion cut solitaire engagement ring onto her finger. Candy looked down at the ring, sparkling in the late afternoon sun, and up at her new fiancé. He leaned in, pulling her toward him, and they kissed for the first time.

A light mist covered them as her lips stayed locked with his. He planted gentle kisses down her décolletage and shoulders. Her chest rose with each one, as his hands proved to be expert in finding all her warm places.

"I finally have you to myself," he said, caressing Candy. "The most sought-after wife on the West Coast."

"Now," Candy blushed, "when you put it like that, it sounds so, so—"

"So what?"

"I may not be the *perfect* wife." She took his hand as they walked to the table with the food and champagne. "But I will always be a professional."

"That's all I ask," he said. As he leaned back in his chair, the sea breeze flapped his linen pants in the wind. His eyes canvassed her face. Another breeze nearly knocked a glass on her lap, and he grabbed it. He then fitted a light shawl that lay beside them over her bare shoulders.

Candy took a deep breath. She loved the safe feeling she had in a man's arms, but Xavier's felt extra protective.

It was a perfect, romantic afternoon spent enjoying champagne and the views, playing the role of a newly engaged couple.

Just before she wondered about the paparazzi, a small boat drifted by in the distance.

"Is that them?" Candy asked as she laid her body against his. "Discreet, it is."

The boat lingered around their perimeter and several paps flashed lights.

"I just made it easy for them," Xavier, whispering in her ears. "By tomorrow, everyone will know."

Candy twisted her body slightly more toward the camera, making sure her ring finger stayed in the front and center. She never made eye contact with the cameras, an amateur move.

They twisted and turned their bodies, enjoying the attention, but more of each other. After a few minutes, Candy nearly forgot about them as she caught herself laughing.

"So, what does a dentist call his photos?" Xavier asked.

"What?" Candy laughed again. He has been making jokes to keep the air light.

He repeated the question again.

"Toothpicks?"

"Okay, you heard that one before."

"I heard all your jokes before. Do you read *Reader's Digest*?"

"I confess. I do. They have the best joke section."

When Candy looked around again, the boat with the paps was gone.

When they returned home that evening, Xavier pulled another bottle of champagne from the refrigerator and led her slowly up the stairs. They entered the master bedroom, and Xavier once again pulled her close. The flirtatious banter she had enjoyed this last week turned into a passionate evening. Xavier was as confident and attentive in bed as he was in business.

His kiss melted her all over again. They kissed each other with a familiarity like they'd done it many times before. His thick, soft lips caressed her ears, then neck, softening her body with every move. She lay back on the bed, pulling him down with her. He crawled on top, his teeth grabbing the edges of her bra straps. She let herself go, arching her back, as he explored every inch of her down to her toes.

9

———————

"Fried or scrambled?" Elena asked Michael as she pulled the eggs out of the fridge. Michael Jr., seven, and Michaela, nine, were already wrapping up their own breakfasts of toast and eggs.

"Mommy, the bus is coming!" Michael Jr. said as he hopped off the chair and wrapped his tiny arms around his mom's legs. She kissed his loose, curly black hair, and his sister grabbed the other side of her. She playfully hugged them back and wished them a good day. She planted two wet kisses on their faces.

"Okay, now, go with Daddy to the bus stop," she said, her heart beating with how much she loved them. Michael gathered them and walked them out.

About ten minutes later, Michael came back. "Fried," he mumbled in his scruffy voice. He sat at the table with his gray sweat suit, broad shoulders hunched over his phone as he drank his coffee. His morning routine consisted of gym, then back home, then real estate office, and then appointments. The morning was the only time Elena got to see him.

The smell of coffee swarmed the kitchen as Elena poured a fresh cup for herself with a dash of cocoa powder. She needed all the caffeine she could handle to get through most mornings. She had never been a morning person, and this morning was proving no different.

Elena had married Michael a few years after she met Candy. The girls-out jaunts together around L.A. came to a stop for a while, but eventually, Elena came back around with late night calls wondering where the marriage went wrong. Elena felt taken for granted sometimes because she had decided to stay home with the kids.

She slathered soft butter on their toast and placed a few slices of ham and olives on the plate. She plopped the eggs, still soft in the middle—the way he liked—on top of the crusty bed. She slid his plate in front of him and sat down to eat hers.

She watched him eat, waiting for him to look at her. She had colored her hair a shade lighter, hoping he'd notice. But nothing, as usual. "How's the food?" she asked.

"Good." He picked up the warm bread with one hand and the phone in the other. Within a minute, he inhaled the food. "Gotta go," he said, wiping the edges of his mouth with a napkin. "You going to the cleaners today?"

"Michael, wait." Elena pushed her plate to the side. "Do you like my hair? I colored it that color you used to like," she said, shaking her tendrils.

"Oh," he said, looking at her, then away quickly. "Okay."

Frustrated, Elena threw up her hands. "Sometimes, I feel like part of the furniture. You don't even pay attention anymore."

He cocked his head to the side, rubbing his overgrown blond beard. "I pay all the bills, you and the kids have nothing to worry about, and you never satisfied. Why?" in his slightly broken, Romanian-accented English.

Elena moved her head from left to right. "We haven't had sex in months—"

"This is about sex?" he interrupted, saying the words in Romanian.

"You know it is not!" Elena exploded back. She hated when he'd talk to her in Romanian. She ran her fingers through her hair, which she decided she would be coloring back to black today. "I need you to stop acting like a father and act like my husband."

Michael leaned in closer to her at the table. "You know, I always thought you married me just to say you were married. I went along with it because, hell, I do love you. I also know that I have given you everything you asked for."

He was right, Elena thought. But that didn't mean it was enough anymore.

Michael had been a car salesman when he arrived from Romania—set up by one of her family members who were already in the States, but since then he had moved from job to job until he landed in feast-or-famine real estate.

"I gave you two kids," Elena said. "I keep you satisfied when you let me. But I need to be happy again. I'm not happy like this."

Michael stood up and grabbed the black gym bag by his feet. "You can't even help yourself. Then how am I supposed to help you?"

That stung Elena.

"Just be happy you're married. You got a husband. Something you always wanted." He grabbed his keys off the table and left.

Elena sat at the table and let Michael's words sink in. She didn't know how to help herself. She didn't know what she needed. Having a friend like Candy was one of the luckiest things that could have happened to her and the worst. Candy helped her in many ways, sometimes financially, but she also showed her what was really possible in the world. That she could find men who would do anything to be with her. That life could be created, stitch by stitch, if one focused hard enough and took risks. Candy was so clear on her needs, and Elena never could quite get a hold of her own.

With her makeup experience from years of doing fashion shows, she started a moderately successful YouTube channel, one that Michael never respected. It was called Makeup Like a Star, where she'd take a celebrity and show viewers how to do exactly the same makeup on their faces. Lately, she had been getting some attention from brands, but she never followed up. She had a backlog of videos and emails.

She rose up from the table and grabbed her phone and a tripod, and started setting herself up. She had a new video in mind, "Makeup Like Viola Davis." Her videos of Black women makeup tutorials did the best. She learned Black women's skin care and makeup from Candy, along with the Black female models she worked with. She was one of the few white makeup artists they demanded to work with.

She walked into the bedroom closet, pulled out her makeup tool-box, and headed back to the kitchen. Then stopped in her tracks.

"Okay." She took a deep breath, sat down, and turned on the camera.

Using her own face, she talked on camera about the steps to take to get the flawless look Viola displayed on any skin. The video lasted six minutes. She stopped it and shut off the camera.

"Great," she sighed, "now instead of eleven, I have twelve videos I need to edit." She put the phone down and felt discouraged again. She didn't feel inspired anymore, and maybe that was it.

With a friend like Candy, Elena always felt not enough.

Candy might praise her real marriage, but Elena craved something more. Candy had found an ingenious way to make her life work, and Elena felt compelled to do the same.

On her way to pick up the kids from school, Elena stopped at the local coffee shop, Mandy's, a neighborhood staple for almost thirty years. She needed another pick-me-up. Instead of the drive-thru, she decided to go inside. As she waited in the line, she spotted Xavier walking in, dressed in tailored blue jeans and a blazer. His face was so buried in his phone, he bumped into someone.

Elena turned back around, pretending not to see him. She felt insanely unprepared in her mom jeans and one of her favorite T-shirts from Target. She didn't know why she felt that way, but she didn't want to embarrass Candy or herself looking a hot mess.

She felt a tap on her shoulder and turned to find Xavier behind her. "Hey," she said, the word sliding out in one long breath.

"Elena, right?" He smiled, putting out his hand to shake hers.

"Nice to see you again," she said, turning her attention quickly to the front of the line, then back to him. "I'm on my way to pick up the kids. What are you doing around *here*?"

"Yeah, I know." He frowned as his phone vibrated in his hands. He glanced at it. "I usually stop by another place near the studio, a little Colombian spot. They make the best coffee. But someone said to check this place out. A little more rustic."

"Right, right." Elena nodded.

He excused himself and turned back to his phone. His fingers frantically texted, making Elena dizzy watching how fast he went.

She turned back around. She heard Xavier on the phone talking in a low voice, laughing lightly. She knew it was Candy.

"So," he said as they both inched ahead in the line. "I got Candy a little something for our wedding. Tell me what you think."

Elena turned around as Xavier pulled out a small blue box.

His face turned serious as he held the box closely to her, keeping it from prying eyes. "So?"

A diamond vine band ring in platinum sparkled so hard Elena blinked repeatedly. She knew it cost at least mid-five figures and thought it was a bit overboard for what he and Candy were actually doing. "It's not really to my taste," Elena said, waving her plain gold band. "But I haven't seen one thing from Tiffany's that Candy doesn't absolutely adore."

Xavier's eyes smiled. He covered the box and slipped it back in his pocket.

"Good," he said, laughing. "Glad I can run it by someone who actually knows her better than I do. Even after the fact."

"Sure, I mean, you can never go wrong with diamonds for a woman," she said. A few people had gotten their orders, and Elena was up next. She ordered, and just as she was about to pay, Xavier said, "Let me get that."

Elena stepped aside as he paid for her order and his own. She thanked him as they both waited for their drinks.

Xavier's phone rang some more as he shifted from one business call to the next. Elena waited a few more extra minutes until her frothy, creamy order of three lattes was ready. She thanked Xavier again, who was still on the phone. He mouthed, "See you soon," as he watched her leave.

Elena sat in her car, happy for Candy. She thought, perhaps Xavier might be the real deal for Candy. But she couldn't help but wonder why a man would drop that much money on a ring when her last car cost about the same. She was terrified of telling anyone what she really needed, in case they said, no. Inside, she felt a roaring river inside her that was hungry, wandering. Her needs scared her sometimes, but she knew they were building, and soon they would overflow.

10

"I see lots of brilliant white everywhere," Brent her publicist said, opening his arms wide. "And diamonds. Shimmery ones ... nothing real. We don't want to incite a riot." He was a former women's studies college professor who spent more time staying up on Hollywood gossip than feminist theory.

Candy gave him the side eye. They were convening in a room that Xavier had transformed into her private office, painted over in shades of teal.

"Oh, not in *that* way," Brent explained quickly. "I mean, Xavier's friends are all civilized. That's what I heard." Brent dug a fork into his fluffy eggs and stuffed them in his mouth. Greta had whipped them up a decadent brunch with waffles, eggs, bacon, and her creamy cappuccinos.

Candy hoped it would keep Brent from talking for a minute.

"This is going to be a simple, elegant affair with less than fifty guests at an upscale resort in Cabo," she said as she scanned the rose garden. The large bay windows in her office always made her feel like she was outside. "We are keeping things small. Is that understood?"

Brent nodded. "I will order invitations and book the venue in the next few days."

"Good. I'll focus on the wedding dress. That will be simple, too." Candy looked at the last piece of waffle on her plate and pushed it to the side. "We only have two weeks left."

Brent's fingers danced across his laptop, recording each of Candy's words.

"Let's focus on the guests," said Candy. "You know who you need there, yes?"

"Yes," Brent said, finally looking up. "And we've already received RSVPs."

"From?"

He clicked open another document. "*Extra, Access Hollywood,* and we have that cute, bubbly reporter from TMZ who is going to be outside, getting you to walk in as if we didn't plan it. I'm playing it like she's the one getting this exclusive shot that even you don't know about. Right outside the venue, just as you come out of the car."

Candy nodded, a bit impressed by his shrewdness. She filled a new plate with strawberries and blueberries and sat back down at the table. "Make sure my sister is invited, not my mother."

Brent gently looked away. "Yes, I understand."

As she listened, Brent went over all the other details.

She interjected, thinking of Marlene and Cleveland's photos on Marlene's show. She wanted to show them they were already old news. "And please make sure *People* publishes those exclusive photos from our engagement the other night."

"They promised they would," Brent said.

"We need a feature on the website, too. Xavier has a new movie coming out. He could use some press that's not about one of his shenanigans."

Brent and Candy gave each other knowing looks. Then Brent's phone rang, and he turned away to pick it up.

His eyes widened, and then he put his hand on his chest.

She nudged his shoulder. *Who is it?* she mouthed.

"Yes, that is fine. We can work with that. Thank you," he said and hung up.

"Work with what?" Candy asked. She wasn't sure why she was smiling as wide as he was.

"That was *People* magazine. They loved the photos so much that they want to do a two-page spread on you and Xavier the day before the wedding. In two weeks."

Candy's mouth dropped. She wanted attention, but this took the cake. She smiled at the thought of Cleveland's jaw hitting the floor when he saw that spread.

LATER THAT EVENING, in her office, Candy did a Google search for everything she could find about herself and Xavier. To her relief, what she found was according to plan. The TMZ website had a barrage of their dating photos, a complete gallery of their relationship. There were videos, too, on different occasions. One of them after lunch on Rodeo, with them walking out of Beets, a popular new lunch spot, as they whisked into Xavier's waiting car. And another of them, on the beach one morning, holding coffees and walking together.

Good, she thought.

She closed the laptop.

When Xavier arrived home, Candy walked down the steps in a cool, easy stride to meet him.

"Hey, you." She smiled, her light brown hair kissing her shoulders. She pressed her body into him until her lips met his.

His muscular arms snaked around her waist, and he ran his hands down her plump backside. He drew her close and then inhaled deeply, breathing in her sweet perfume.

"You're home early," she said, taking his hand as they walked to the living room.

"Shit was getting too intense on the set today. Sometimes, the men are worse than the women." He poured himself a snifter of Hennessey at the bar. "I swear, I'm like two minutes away from punching one of those sons of bitches."

"Who?" She settled on the sofa and draped one long, shapely leg over the other.

"Sandy Levy. The fuck." He sat down on the white couch across the room, directly facing her. "He didn't show up today."

"Xavier, you know Levy is the highest paid actor there is. Everything he's in is a blockbuster hit. He's worth a few headaches."

He scoffed. "It's me. They don't respect me."

Candy picked up a few cues about how Xavier ticked. He had an eagerness to please, along with a determination to get everything he wants. No matter the costs. Even sacrificing himself. "Xavier, you're going to have to table that thought. I learned something new today. We have *People* magazine coming. *Here.* To interview us, the day before our wedding."

"What for?" He frowned.

Candy couldn't help but be irritated. "What do you mean 'what for'?"

"I mean, what's the plan?"

"Well, I thought you'd never ask." She pulled out her phone. "Here's us on People. I'm sure your publicist shared this with you?" She wanted to focus his attention. "Folks want to get to know us. *People* magazine will help them do that. So, you'll have to do more than stand around and look handsome. You'll have to do most of the talking, to appear calm, relaxed. Give brief answers. Look at me when you talk. Use words like 'now or never' and 'real.' It builds urgency and sounds authentic."

"Urgency?"

Candy sighed. She hoped Xavier would be in step. "We need them to know that you are excited about getting married. A fresh start. New you. Blah, blah."

Xavier looked doubtful, but not for the reason she expected. "Can they do it when we return?"

"Why?"

"I got so much work, Candy. With this new movie, I'm running past deadline. The wedding." He held his hands up. "We can't possibly fit all this in."

Candy drew in a deep breath, getting impatient. "Is it too much for you?"

Alerted by her sharp tone, Xavier watched her carefully.

"It's going to be a long road, Xavier. You're not exactly Prince Charming in Hollywood."

"Yeah, okay, Candy. You don't have to rub it in."

"You should get your money's worth out of me." Candy sauntered over to the bar to fix herself a drink. She felt his gaze on her from the back. "And make it worth *my* time."

He walked up behind her, eyeing her fitted purple bodycon dress. I'm sorry," he said, coming down a few notches in his tone. Candy's self-assured confidence tone calmed him. "Maybe I'm just tired." He rested his hand on her trim waist.

She poured herself a shot of Grand Marnier and spun around on her heels to face him. "You just follow my lead."

CANDY BARELY SLEPT the days before the *People* magazine interview. Pressure at work and the wedding preparations had Xavier chasing his tail around. Amidst all of that, he kept up his part. Taking Candy out on dates, buying her flowers, and being the doting fiancé.

Elena had arrived early to do her makeup. Candy trusted no one else. She also knew that Elena was unhappy at home and slacking on her YouTube channel. She hoped that including Elena like this would help her focus on sharing her skills with the world again.

The *People* interview crew arrived with much to-do. Xavier offered the crew a few of his suggestions about aspects of the staging. He wanted them to film with the fireplace at the background, and the fresh flowers he had bought her to shower the background, that scented the air and bought a feel of romance to the room.

During the interview, Xavier followed all of Candy's cues. At one point, Xavier got tongue tied, when the reporter, a young, blonde woman with a pink streak in her hair, asked him, "What is true happiness for you?"

Xavier stammered. "I don't know. I mean. It depends on what you define as happiness."

That reporter repeated the question in a different way. "How do you define it as?"

"What we mean is that happiness is what we *both* make it," Candy said, smoothly covering for him.

The reporter looked relieved, so did Xavier, as she moved on to other questions.

Candy knew that in these interviews the reporter was interested in talking to the star, but Candy still managed to get in a few words. This was her most high-profile marriage, and she wasn't going to be able to fly as much under the radar as before.

Their photos, which included locations all over Xavier's lavish estate, were shots for the ages. Candy changed three times with Elena changing her look dramatically each time. "You look ravishing in every shot," Xavier said, as the day wrapped. "Just flawless."

"Thanks to Elena," she said, watching from the front steps as everyone left.

Xavier and Candy waved as Elena drove off in her tattered, nineties mini-van.

11

———

Cabo had turned into Candy's favorite wedding site. It was away from all the noise, a setting for an intimate but grand destination wedding. Xavier invited only his parents, several industry people, and his neighbors. Lettie came, too, dressed in one of Candy's vintage Chanel midi dresses. It bothered her when people asked about her family, so she was grateful to have Elena and Lettie by her side.

Elena was standing behind her, struggling with her zipper. "Did you gain a few pounds over the last week?"

"It's Greta," Candy replied. "I don't know if she's deliberately trying to fatten me up or what. That Italian woman can cook anyone out of their own kitchen!"

As soon as Candy laughed, Elena made a final tug and zipped the dress all the way. "Whew," she mumbled under her breath.

A knock on the door startled them. In just a few minutes, the wedding would start, and she hadn't met anyone from Xavier's family. She'd told herself to wait after the wedding. Too many questions, too many assumptions could ruin the flow. She wanted everything to stay calm.

A dark brown woman with glowing skin, cropped hair, and a

yellow dress stood on the other side of the door. When she saw Candy, she smiled.

"Honey, you look beautiful! Do you have a minute? I'm Xavier's mom, Nora."

The woman glided into the room and threw her arms around Candy. She returned the hug cautiously. "How are you, Mrs. Oshun? I've heard so much about you."

It wasn't a complete lie. Xavier did give her a brief rundown, but at almost forty, Candy's brain wasn't retaining what it used to.

"Oh yes? Like what?" Mrs. Oshun gazed at her with curious eyes.

"Meet my friend, Elena. Elena, Nora," Candy said, hoping to buy a few moments to jar her memory.

"How was your flight?" Elena asked.

"Wonderful. Xavier always makes sure I travel in style."

The door opened, and Lettie walked in. "Everything looks set," she said.

"Oh, meet Xavier's mom. This is my sister Lettie."

"She's just as beautiful," his mother cooed.

Lettie blushed, and said, "I'll be outside with everyone else. Nice meeting you." She left as quietly as she came in.

"You must be enjoying retirement," Candy said, rejoining the conversation. "I heard you just got back from Cuba."

"Oh," Nora said, slightly blushing. "I guess my son does know I exist. Yes, it was glorious. Me and a few girlfriends are enjoying our best years. And by the way, baby, you look so exquisite. Like a black Barbie doll." She hugged Candy again. "I'll leave you two be," she said. "See you after the ceremony."

"What was that about?" Elena asked. "Mothers-in-law. Ugh."

Candy remembered the agony Michael's mother had put her through when her son left Romania to be with Elena. Candy glanced at the clock. "Oh, look at the time, Elena."

A few of the resort assistants hurried into the room to attend to Candy's last-minute needs. Then the music began.

The paparazzi flashed several lights in her face as soon as she stepped out of her villa. Elena took Candy by the arm and escorted her to the beach. A simple stretch of rose petals lined a path before them. Slowly, Elena proceeded to walk Candy down the aisle, just as she had done at her last wedding. She would never put Lettie under this kind of scrutiny, but Elena enjoyed it as much as she did.

As Candy walked, her eyes swept across the small group of people who had gathered. As their eyes locked with hers, some acknowledged her with nods, some with cheers, and some with question marks. After all, to them she was a woman who had popped up out of nowhere and was now marrying one of the wealthiest directors in Hollywood. Lettie, sat upfront, alone, with a tense look. Candy could tell she wished their mom was there. Lettie may be feeling alone with all this glitz, she thought. And with what she had to do, she didn't know if she could give her sister the attention she needed today.

Candy fixed her smile on Xavier. His long, lean body was draped in a white suit with black trim. His hands were gently folded in front of him, legs slightly apart and his shoulders back. He looked every bit the strong, dignified African warrior.

Her heart fluttered.

He must have noticed because his eyes softened as she came closer.

The ceremony lasted only a short while, with traditional vows and a kiss at the end. A helicopter hovered over them. She gave Xavier a reassuring smile.

Even though it was her day, Candy made the afternoon about charming each and every guest. Everyone had questions for her, which she answered as warmly and kindly as she could.

"You know," said a man holding a plate of bacon-crusted shrimp in his hand. His name was Vince, and he was a childhood friend of Xavier's. "Not to be in bad taste or nothing, but I never thought Xavier would get married. He was like the Leonardo DiCaprio of the crew. Always had so many chicks. You must be one special woman."

Before she could respond, the woman he was with—a blonde with glaring red lips and a white dress—said, "How can I get my Vince to do the same?"

Candy gave her a small smile. "As a matter of fact, I'll let Xavier answer this himself. Xavier!" she called.

A few heads turned. Xavier was taking a call on his cell, but he hung up and walked right over.

"Vince, and his lady, want to know what made you settle down," she said with a smirk, knowing the secret between them.

Xavier laughed, picking up a glass of champagne. "Uhm," he gave Candy a quizzical look, "Candy is the first woman I would do anything for," he said, pulling her to him and landing a kiss on her lips. After a few moments, Candy excused herself.

Her eyes followed Lettie as she filled her plate at the one of the several delectable food tables. "Hey, my love," she said, approaching her. She slipped her arms into hers as they walked together to a nearby table.

"So, what do you think?" Candy asked.

"Congratulations." Lettie put her plate down and thanked God. "Everything is so elegant, and I love that this one is in Cabo. It makes me want to travel more. I just wish—"

"You wish Mommy was here, right?" Candy lowered her eyes to meet her sister's, but she was staring into her shrimp and caviar.

"Mommy was livid that I came to this wedding."

"Too bad. If she knew how to act and not embarrass me, I might have invited her. She's a time bomb."

Lettie shook her head in disbelief. "It's like she has this anger for you. I can't describe it."

"Please don't. Not today."

Lettie smiled. "I wasn't going to let her stop me from today."

"What happened to the guy you were seeing? We would have paid for him to come with you all this way."

"Well, I don't really know him well enough to invite him."

Candy wondered if this guy could be the catalyst to get Lettie to go to college full-time. "Lettie, if you lived on campus, that would probably help your relationship with him. Does he treat you good?"

"Yes, he is so patient. I have canceled on him many times. I do like him. He is pre-med and seems to come from a nice family. I don't know why he is interested in me."

"Why wouldn't he be?"

Lettie blushed again.

Candy was aware that Lettie hadn't grown into her fullness yet, but she would. Like her older sister, she was a late bloomer.

"What if I paid for your college, so you can stay on campus?"

Lettie seemed to expand at Candy's suggestion. She sat up straighter and flashed the biggest smile Candy hadn't seen in a while. "I'd like that."

"I knew you would," Candy said as she picked a shrimp from Lettie's place. "I'll get things set up. Just send me the bursar info."

After a few moments passed, Lettie spoke. "Can I ask something?"

"When have I ever said no to that?"

"How do you keep going through all this?"

"It's my job, Lettie." Candy gave her sister a kiss on the cheek and walked away to greet the other guests.

12

———————

"Fuck me!" Xavier shouted, just a day back from Cabo. He threw his cell phone down on the bed.

Candy rolled over, the covers draped over her naked body. She brought her hand to her forehead to keep the sun from blinding her. It was a bright February morning, and they were officially Mr. and Mrs. Oshun.

"What?" Candy moaned, hoping to get some more sleep. With their constant lovemaking, she hadn't been able to catch more than a few hours straight.

"We got some place to be," Xavier said, hopping out of bed. He slipped on a pair of boxers that lay on the floor, neatly folded.

"Who was on the phone?"

"Alex, my assistant at the studio. She reminded me that there is this huge cocktail party tonight. I should have told you, but I honestly thought we wouldn't make it because of the wedding. But we have to go."

"Who will be there?"

"All the major financiers, and of course all the top producers and agents. It's a who's-who. I *need* to be there."

Candy raised her body up on the bed and gazed at her reflection in the mirror. Her hair was matted, her almond skin was slightly sunburned, and she was drained. "Is there anyone there I need to know?"

"Everyone," he said matter-of-factly as he slipped into a freshly ironed T-shirt and pristine white sneakers. His eyes lit up his face. "I can't wait until they meet you. You're going to be the most beautiful wife in the room full of the usual."

"The usual?"

"Yeah, white women. But be careful, they can be quite catty when a beautiful Black woman is in the room."

"Oh, I'm used to that. The envy in their eyes could kill."

He bent down and kissed her lips, still with a trace of matted lipstick from the night before. "What do you think would be good to wear?"

"I'll wear the gray platinum gown, and you can wear your gray suit."

"Cool, I'll have my assistant get our clothes ready. Anything else you need?" he asked, waiting patiently.

Candy softened her eyes and reached for him. She couldn't explain it, but she felt pulled to Xavier more than she had expected in the last few weeks. He was good to her. "No, you've been great."

He planted a few more kisses along her arm. "I'm going for a run. When I get back, will you be ready for breakfast?"

"If it's one of Greta's breakfasts, yes." Candy rolled back over and pulled the covers to her chin.

WHEN CANDY and Xavier walked into The Lorraine ballroom, her heart skipped a beat. The place was like a fairy tale, with gold and silver trimmings, a horde of high-class executives—bubbly, statuesque women, handsome, robust men. Candy's smooth, regal presence and Xavier's relaxed style lifted the room to another level as the only Black couple in the room. Her eyes perused the room, seeing if anyone interesting caught her eye to get to know. Until she found it.

Cleveland and Marlene. She darted her attention back to business, though miffed that her evening already felt ruined.

"This is Ethan Huffman," Xavier said as he introduced Candy to one of his biggest financiers. "Ethan, meet my lovely new wife, Candy."

"Candy, great to meet you," Ethan said, giving her a generous handshake. "The world now knows you 'as the luckiest wife in Hollywood.' Thanks to *People* magazine."

"Well, I like to think of Xavier as the luckiest man in the world," Candy said, glowing inside the gold organza dress she'd decided on instead. She switched it at the last minute to complement her tan.

Ethan's cheeks flush with red.

He took her hand and kissed it. "You are absolutely more stunning in person," he said, winking at Xavier. "How did you end up with her?"

Xavier looked embarrassed for a moment. "Call me *lucky*, I guess," he said.

"And," Candy interjected, putting her arm through Xavier's. "I have never met a more dedicated man than Xavier. We take good care of each other."

"Ah." Ethan leaned in and asked, "You have any sisters?"

Lettie would never be interested in you, she thought to herself.

Ethan smiled. "Excuse me. Nice meeting you both, but I have to run now and catch up with my wife." He gave Xavier another wink, and then he was gone.

THROUGHOUT THE EVENING, Xavier and Candy made their rounds. To Candy, the wives all seemed to be gadgets of a sort. Gadgets that never failed to shine and sparkle when prompted. Candy understood. The men were the real players in Hollywood. And no movie got made on merit alone. This was far different from the NBA scene Candy had experienced with Greg, where older wives dominated their younger men, or where very young wives were just learning the ropes. This room was full of she-wolves. They looked quiet, but they could bite.

While Xavier entrenched himself in conversation with a colleague, Candy made her way to the champagne fountain. She hadn't seen one of those since the eighties, she thought, looking at it flow up, down, and around.

She felt a brush against her shoulder. "Still love your champagne, I see," Cleveland said as she filled her glass with the shimmery concoction.

"Cleveland," Candy said in a curt tone. She turned her back to him.

Speaking from behind her, he said, "You looked stunning on your wedding day. More beautiful than I could ever imagine. I am truly happy for you."

Candy brought the glass to her lips, ignoring him.

Cleveland came around to face her. "I really am. I just hope you won't throw me away."

"You threw *us* away. Or any possibility with your latest, uh, pick or whatever she is."

Cleveland's face blanched in surprise.

Candy knew she had hurt him. Her eyes locked in with his. She still felt him a part of her. "How could you? Out of all the women in the world. Marlene? You could do better."

"I didn't think the office was the right place to tell you about Marlene—"

"It's fine," she said, cutting him off midway. "I'm fine."

Cleveland's eyes softened toward her. He could read her as well as anyone. "Forgive me."

Candy crossed her arms and maintained eye contact with him.

"Candy, I've been thinking—"

"Please don't think. It got us this far," Candy said, looking around the room suddenly.

All the while Marlene had been watching from the cocktail lounge area, doing a bad job of not paying attention to their exchange.

Candy didn't care until she spotted Xavier glancing in her direction, too. The last thing she wanted was for him to approach. Thankfully, a colleague guided him to meet a group of people in another room.

"I will always be here for you, Candy," Cleveland finally said, standing so close to her.

She moved her shoulders toward him, feeling the chemistry they used to share.

"No one can ever change what we had. Or," he cleared his throat, "or have."

"Have?" Candy titled her head to the side. "So, you just want it all?"

"That's not what I mean. You'll see."

Just when Candy thought Cleveland might say something intimate, Marlene walked up, dressed garishly in a sequined purple and green dress. Inappropriate, Candy thought. Was this really the best Cleveland could do?

"Oh, honey. If I have to wear these Louboutins for another minute, I'm gonna die," Marlene croaked in her loud voice that didn't seem to be any different than the one she had on TV.

"Candy, this is Marlene. Marlene, Candy."

Candy made a closed-mouth smile. "Marlene."

"Hello, Ms. Candy. Looking ever as ravishing as the day you came into town. How long ago was that?"

"Excuse me?" Candy asked, baffled at first by Marlene's sarcasm. Then she dismissed Marlene with a laugh. Sure, she'd been around for a while, but she had a hell of a lot to show for it.

"We're just about to leave," said Cleveland, grabbing Marlene by both elbows and ushering her away. "Marlene, you had too much to drink. Good night, Candy."

Candy watched them head off, feeling a pang of pity for Cleveland.

Eventually, she found Xavier in the parlor room next door.

"Everything okay?" he asked in a low tone. He pulled her in by the waist.

She flipped her hair to one side. "Couldn't be better," she said, doing her best to sound like it.

He kissed her ear and whispered, "I need to meet him." He nodded in the direction of a slim Asian man with blond hair and thick black bifocals. "But he hates me. I haven't been able to get his interest in this next film I need to do to extend my contract. If I don't get that money, I lose money."

Candy was instantly alert. She was in her element. "Has the production company reached out to him on your behalf?" she said.

"Yes, and it was so embarrassing," Xavier said, talking lower now. "He says that if I'm directing the film, he won't do it. But I have a feeling he wants me to reach out first."

"Then why don't you?" Candy replied. "I've seen him look at you several times tonight. Even now."

"I'm not begging."

"Is he gay?"

"Yes, and I think that's part of it. But I've gotten this far without bending over, and I don't expect to start now," Xavier huffed.

Candy gauged his mood, sensing his dilemma. "Thankfully, you have me."

Xavier narrowed his eyes as Candy smiled. "What are you thinking?"

She turned her back on him and faced the room. "Is that pretty redhead his wife?"

"Yes, well, his beard."

"Watch this," Candy said, gliding over to the other side of the ballroom and leaving Xavier looking on. Elegantly dodging waiters and their heavily plated trays of food and champagne-filled glasses, she slowed down a few times for friendly nods and glances.

"Are you Darcy Allen?" Candy asked the red-haired woman with the pale skin and green eyes.

Darcy turned from the crowd she had been talking to and slowly extended her hand. "Candy?"

"Yes, nice to see you again." Candy flashed a smile. "Didn't we meet briefly at Tracy Anderson's Pilates studio?"

"Yes, I just didn't expect to see you here," Darcy said with a nervous smile. Then her voice grew terse.

"Oh?" Candy asked with not the slightest hint of the annoyance she felt. She learned early to never show her hand to strangers.

"I just thought you and Xavier would still be awash in wedding bliss," she said.

"Would you have time for a glass of wine next week?" Candy said, taking back control of the conversation.

Darcy's eyebrows rose, making her already big eyes, bigger. "Candy, I know what you're trying to do. If you weren't as beautiful as you are, I'd say no. But I want to get to know you. How's Tuesday?" she asked, shooting Candy a smoldering look.

Candy caught that look and wasn't sure what to make of it. "Tuesday it is."

"And one thing, Candy. I know you're into Xavier and all, but he has a hot temper. He threw his boot at a young actress last year and bruised her face. That stopped production in its tracks. Just know that."

Candy swallowed her shock. "See you next week," she said and walked back to Xavier.

"So?" he said.

"It went good. We're having wine."

Candy grabbed a freshly poured glass of champagne and brought it to her lips.

"How'd you know her?" he asked.

"I did my research. She, like many of the wives, goes to Tracy's studio. I signed up there weeks ago. This was an easy catch. But I have a feeling it will get harder from here."

Candy guzzled her entire glass at once.

13

Elena arrived back home after Candy's Cabo wedding on a natural high. The food, the ambiance, and her exquisite hotel suite were more than she had asked. Candy even gifted her round-trip tickets and a ten-day stay at the same resort for her and Michael to enjoy anytime. Michael hadn't gone to the wedding because he had to go to a closing.

She checked on Michaela and Michael Jr. upstairs.

"Need anything, guys?" she asked as they both did their homework.

"I'm helping Michael with his math," said Michaela, teasingly poking Michael with a pen.

Elena smiled and closed the door. She put her ears to it and did hear them working. Though she wasn't sure how much help Michaela could be, she always checked their homework to be sure. She was proud of how smart her children were. She just hoped to give them a better life.

As she sat at the kitchen table, she eyed the tickets on her cell phone. She had planned to tell Michael about them with hopes that it could be a way to reignite the passion in their marriage.

After a few minutes, she heard Michael come in through the front door. Something he rarely did. He always used the garage. He also rarely came home this early.

She waited for him to come to the kitchen. His face looked drawn and flattened with despair. She didn't say a word.

He threw himself down on a chair. He looked at her as he scrubbed his thin, blondish beard with his fingers. "We need to talk."

Elena had heard these words a hundred times. Even so, she listened as Michael told her he had been fired at the real estate office due to his low sales. The last closing, a small, underpriced condo, didn't meet his quota. They were throwing his best leads to younger people in his office as a way to edge him out. It was always someone else's fault, she thought.

He bought a hand to his head. "We need to figure something out."

Elena was frustrated, furious that he had been fired. *Again*. She paused, remembering what they both might need.

"What if we went away, took a trip, cleared our minds? Maybe if we did that, we both could get back on our feet and decide what we want to do."

He looked at her like she was speaking a different language.

"Candy gave us this," she said, pulling up the tickets and pictures of the resort.

Michael took her phone, scrolled through the information more closely, and handed it back to her. "No," he said.

"Why not? You have the time now. And we can leave the kids at your mom's house for a week. They'll be fine."

Michael clenched his jaw together so tightly she could see the little muscles in them. "You'd do anything not to work."

"This is a *free* trip. F–r–e–e."

"I'm not talking about a free trip. You can't live off other people forever. You got to get a job." The last few words came out slowly. "That's the plan."

Elena put down her phone. Her not having a full-time job had been an issue for them since the kids were born. He did not respect her YouTube efforts, even though she managed to bring home enough to pay for groceries and gas. "Michael, I'm not ready yet. I really feel if I had your help, we can make some serious money together."

"Is online going to pay for our kids' health insurance? Our health insurance? What about retirement?" he said, his voice growing. He leaped out of the chair. "I'm done. You figure out how you're going to make this work. I need a break," he said and left.

Elena sat with her mouth wide open. She did not have a high school diploma or even a real certification in cosmetology. Everyone called her naturally talented. Candy was the only one who encouraged her to formalize her training to get higher-paying gigs. That is, Candy was the only one who took her talent seriously.

Elena looked over her shoulder. The kids stood at the bottom of the steps, alerted by their father's shouting.

"Ahh, honies," Elena said, calming them down. She wiped the tears from both of their round, soft faces and took their tiny hands to the kitchen. "Here's a few snacks. Go back upstairs, finish your homework, and Mommy will help you get ready for dinner, okay?"

They each took a packet of their favorite gummy bears and ran back up to their rooms.

Michael wanted her to take an office desk job. Something predictable and reliable. He wanted her to do what he wouldn't do himself. And that's what enraged her the most. When she figured that Michael was safely tucked away in his man cave basement, she called Candy.

Elena didn't want to start up with her problems right away. She and Candy chatted about her running into Xavier at Mandy's and his parents coming for lunch soon at the house.

She waited for Candy to finish. "I got a problem."

"Who did it?" Candy joked.

That made Elena laugh a little. "Guess who?"

Candy's silence spoke loudly about who she guessed it was.

"He lost his job again. And he is demanding that I support the family. You know I'm not ready yet."

Candy listened, and Elena knew she wanted to hear her out before volunteering anything.

"You know I have always wanted to work for myself. And my YouTube videos are really catching on. I need more time."

Candy cleared her throat and listened some more.

Then Elena broke down. Tears welled up in the corners of her eyes. "I'm so scared, Candy. I can't do this. I can't even talk to him. He doesn't listen."

"Honey, the ball is in your court. He just told you what he needed. What do you need?"

Elena thought about it for a moment. "My own money would be nice."

"That's right," Candy said. "Just think about not having to ask him for a dime. Being able to stash your own cash."

"But how? I don't have any skills besides makeup. I'd love to do makeup again in a real way."

"Elena, if you really want a job, then I can help you. I can ask Xavier if he has anything on his set. You're one of the few white makeup artists who really knows Black skin."

Elena's face lit up. "Would you? Could you let me know? I mean if it is not asking too much."

"Elena, you are my girl. I'd do anything for you. Give me a few days."

Elena's stomach tingled with excitement. She could picture herself on a movie set working on Viola Davis or even Meryl Streep. Xavier worked with the best, and that was exactly what she needed.

14

Candy hadn't met with Darcy yet, though they had been in touch via text messages. Neither had mentioned Darcy's comments about Xavier's temper after the cocktail party. Candy knew better to keep private details private. She thought about what Darcy might want from her, too. But she wasn't worried. In her book, at the end, everyone wanted to be liked. This bought to mind Charlotte Stonewall, the wife of Fletcher Stonewall, a partner at Cleveland's firm. She was a bigwig's wife she had to finesse. For the life of her, she didn't know what Charlotte, a well-respected, seventy-year-old woman, had against them both, especially Cleveland, other than being Black. But even that seemed too basic for Charlotte. Come to find out, it was actually nothing. Charlotte had no friends and felt offended that Candy had not made an extra effort to get to know her. And the unwritten rule in the office was that Charlotte Stonewall ran things, even though her husband's name was on the mantel. She herself was a successful attorney who no longer practiced, preferring a life of leisure. Candy spent months getting Charlotte to accept her invites for lunch, dinner. Until finally she did. They became quick friends, and Cleveland's career soared at the firm, becoming a top partner and receiving accolades and cases even he marveled over.

Charlotte became his biggest advocate. It had also become en vogue to have Black friends with the country celebrating its own Black, powerful leaders. Candy's timing and persistence was perfect. Until Charlotte's death, they had remained close.

Today, Xavier's parents were coming for lunch. Candy and Xavier had been finding their rhythm. So far, she ran the relationship. But slowly, she had noticed Xavier asserting himself more, like a real husband. She had to be careful about that. Still, she liked it.

"Are you ready?" Candy called as she emerged from the powder room fully dressed for brunch. She wore a white sheath dress, flats, and had swept her hair up into a demure bun.

Xavier was one of those men who could make any clothes look good. He stood in one of his traditional, African white linen numbers that had been fitted to drape his body to perfection. He slipped on his Rolex—and then froze when he saw her. "Damn, Candy. You look good enough to eat." He raised her dress to her hips and then edged her toward the bed.

"Can we save something for later?" she whispered. She looked at his watch. "Your parents should be here in about ten minutes."

He sighed, gently massaging her shoulders as they gazed in the mirror at each other. He nuzzled the skin of her neck with his nose, sending tingles throughout her body. Then he said, "I may have to head back to the studio tonight. Can I get some before I go?"

"When your parents *leave*." She laughed. Slowing the heat down between their bodies, she turned to face him. "How are things on the set going?" She hadn't heard him talk about work for a few days.

"No news is good news," he said flatly. "We're just into the first few weeks of shooting. Staying under budget." He sat on the edge of the bed, watching as Candy went to the closet to grab a few more bracelets.

"You remember Elena, right?" she asked.

"Yeah, I bumped into her at Mandy's."

"She told me," Candy said. "And I had a talk with her the other night. She's one of the best makeup artists I know, Xavier."

"And?" he asked, looking at her with a raised eyebrow.

"Do you need an extra hand on set?"

Xavier folded his hands as he thought for a bit. "Are you asking me to hire her?"

Candy slid next to him on the edge of the bed. "She wants to keep her skills fresh. Get her name back out there." Candy didn't want to reveal the real reasons, wary of divulging too much about her friend.

Xavier considered it. "Candy, I don't know. I mean, Nick and his team do all the makeup. I'm not sure how they would feel."

Candy moved her body closer to him until he fully embraced her again.

"Let me think about it," he said. "Does she know I don't take any bull? I'm the boss from her wildest dreams."

"She's a strong Romanian woman. She can handle it."

As if on cue, his phone beeped with a message from the butler that his parents had arrived.

"They're early," Xavier said, sliding his phone in his pocket. They both snapped back into neutral positions. "Are we on the same page today?" he asked.

"As long as you are cool."

"They're going to ask you about kids. They're Nigerian. They can't help it."

"I can handle that."

THE AFTERNOON STARTED SLOW. Mrs. and Mr. Oshun, Xavier's parents, were quieter than Candy expected, studying and analyzing with their eyes her every move and word. She wondered if they knew who she really was, she thought. But that was impossible.

A bevy of fruit, smoked salmon, grilled shrimp, croquettes, waffles, salad, and slices of baked ham adorned the deck that overlooked Xavier's estate.

"Have you guys discussed a family?" asked Xavier's father out of the blue. He looked like a spitting image of Xavier, only twenty years older. He looked at Xavier. "You know this world can't have enough beautiful Black families."

"We're leaving it in God's hands," said Candy, fidgeting with her bracelets. She prayed that they'd drop it.

Xavier's father was about to say more, but then his mom jumped in. "Oh, that is so romantic," she cooed. "But at your age, Candy, you should not be waiting. God is waiting on us, too."

A bead of sweat ran down the back of Candy's neck. She rubbed it. "But—"

"Do you believe in God?" Xavier's father bellowed in a deep voice.

"Yes," Candy said, straightening her back. She hadn't felt this flustered in a while. She shot Xavier a look, who kept his eyes on his parents. She wondered at his silence.

His father continued. "I waited for this day that my baby boy would have a wife. Lord, thank you for blessing our son with this gorgeous, loving woman." He gazed up at the sky with opened arms, so did his mother as they both clasped their hands.

Candy smiled lightly, masking her guilt. It was the perfect time to change the subject, she thought. "Xavier told me you guys were planning a trip to Zanzibar."

"Oh yes, I love going," Xavier's mother replied. "Our lovely son booked us a whole month out there with shopping, cruising—"

"It's going to be great," Xavier's father said, slicing into a piece of ham. "One day, I want to take a trip with all of Xavier's children. Yes?" His father patted Xavier on the back.

"You have to start soon," his mother warned, nodding at Candy.

"Well, Xavier has so many projects planned. Right, Xavier?"

Xavier stopped chewing and swallowed whatever he had. "We can make time. At some point."

Candy tried again. "Oh, I have several friends there who own the Dembe restaurant. It's the best place in town. They will treat you like royalty if you go to Zanzibar."

"We have been there," said Xavier's mother, frowning. Candy wondered where the nice woman she met on her wedding day went.

"It would be nice for all of us to go one day. Did Xavier tell you our family is a family of many children. I am the daughter of eleven, and Xavier father is son of fifteen."

"We have a tradition of big families," Xavier said.

Candy seethed inside as he joined in on the coup. "Well, that's nice."

"So, you only have one sister. Wow, that is hard," Xavier's father said, in a whispering tone. "Your mother had no sons?"

"No, just us girls," Candy said, careful to keep her tone even. It was killing her not to throw the whole table over on them.

"I'm sure you want to give our son, many sons," his father chuckled, his fatty cheeks rounding on his face.

"I'm not ready." Candy managed a smile, as she looked at Xavier. She remembered what he warned her.

"Not ready? Ey!" His mother yelped and muttered a few Igbo words to his father.

Xavier looked at Candy and smiled back.

15

"How are you liking Hollywood so far? You and Xavier, frankly, have one of the most enviable estates," Darcy said as she sprinkled salt and pepper on her artichoke salad. They were sitting outside a downtown Italian café on a cool, breezy afternoon.

"It's different from the rest of L.A., for sure." Candy idly watched the tourists that passed, one with a T-shirt that read "I did the best I could."

"That's not the only thing that's a lot better." Darcy batted her eyes at Candy from across the table.

Candy thought Darcy was the worst flirt, but if acting receptive could help to get closer to her, she'd entertain it to a point. She'd been with another woman while married to Greg. For a few nights in Antigua, a local woman, ten years older, had befriended her at the hotel bar. Greg had his fun that week, and she did, too. But Darcy wasn't exactly her type. "So, the other night. What you said about my husband..."

"Forget that. I had too much champagne." Darcy waved her fork in the air as a couple of children ran between the tables. "More Moet, more problems."

Candy wasn't ready to let it drop. "So it wasn't true?"

"It was true. I was just way out of line."

Candy didn't want to appear as if she knew nothing about Xavier and his rumored ways. "Thanks for being so open with me, Darcy," she said. "But how did you know I wouldn't slap you in the face?"

"You don't seem like that type," Darcy said, chewing her salad slowly.

"Well, Xavier isn't that type either, anymore. One thing I love about him is that he knows he's not perfect. He's a man who has literally done a one-eighty in his life. He's good to me."

"He owes the studio millions. Why do you think he wants Ben on board?"

Candy thought it made more sense now, his insistence on meeting Ben. "Has Ben had a conversation with Xavier?"

Darcy remained silent, pretending to eat. She put her fork down at last.

"What if we invite you two over for dinner?" said Candy. "I know Xavier would love it. We can all get to know each other better."

Darcy's eyebrows rose.

Candy couldn't read her face, but she had to be sure. "OK?"

"What if I want to get to know *you* better?" Darcy stuck her finger in her champagne and sucked the tip.

"Let's start with dinner first."

Darcy pulled out her cell phone to check. "We got an opening next Thursday at eight. Your place?"

"Yes, our place. Do you have any allergies I should know of?"

"Nope, we eat *everything*."

Darcy and Ben arrived right on time. Xavier had the dinner catered by one of Ben's favorite restaurants, Edward's. That was Candy's idea after reading Ben's mention of it in an interview in *Vanity Fair*.

Edward's Steakhouse was known for its thousand-dollar burger and twenty-four-carat gold truffle fries. Candy had ordered the most expensive main dishes, sides, salads, and desserts. There was not one bad dish at Edward's.

As they sat around the table, Ben wiped his mouth with a napkin, then said, "You guys have no idea that I've been trying to get to Edward's for months. Ask Darcy. Every time we had a plan, something fell through, and we couldn't go."

"Exactly," Darcy said. "How'd you know it was Ben's favorite?" She turned to Candy.

"Well, Xavier mentioned it to me."

"Ahh," said Ben, looking up from his filet mignon. "Xavier, I have to apologize. My lovely wife convinced me to come tonight. I didn't want to."

Xavier looked on with a closed-mouth smile. Candy prayed he'd keep it that way.

"I never liked you," Ben went on. "I thought you were just another irresponsible, know–it-all hothead director who thinks his shit doesn't stink."

Xavier's frozen smile faded by the second.

Candy shot Ben a look that told him to back off, and Darcy winced.

"But you really seem like a stand-up guy though. I didn't give myself a chance to get to know you. So, I hope we can start." Ben flashed a handsome smile.

All eyes turned to Xavier, and he didn't let Candy down.

Xavier's face relaxed. "No problem, man. I know how the industry is. I'm all about getting to know how people are on the inside. Fuck what other people say about them."

"Right, right," Ben said. "We should discuss a few things then?"

"Definitely." Xavier nodded in a way that showed he was confident that the rest of the evening would go well.

After dinner, they gathered in the den for cocktails. The night continued with conversation and industry banter and plenty of gossip about who was sleeping with whom, and who was sleeping with all the wrong people. Candy didn't have much to add. She just listened.

Then Darcy walked over and sat down next to her. Candy had

kicked off her heels long ago, and Darcy commented, "You have the prettiest, daintiest feet. What size are you?"

"A six," Candy said, watching as Ben and Xavier disappeared into the library.

Darcy ran her hands from Candy's knee to her slim ankle. "Your legs are the sexiest. Do you wax or shave?"

"Wax," Candy said, slightly impressed by the smooth, feather-light touch Darcy delivered.

Darcy put her drink down. She picked up Candy's right foot, rested it on her lap, and gave it tender, firm strokes.

Candy's closed her eyes slightly, relaxing into Darcy's soothing strokes. Darcy coddled her toes and pressed firmly into the bottom of her soles.

"Mmm, I can tell you've walked a mile in these babies." Darcy giggled, her shoulders getting into it. She gently led Candy's foot between her legs. Darcy jutted her hips forward, pressing Candy's big toe on the fleshy part between her thighs. She put a light pressure on it. Darcy moved her hips forward some more.

Candy watched as Darcy's eyes rolled back. She did everything she could to hide laughing at her foot being used to get Darcy off. At last, she decided to break the spell when Darcy pressed her foot in her farther. Candy slid down the couch a bit and asked, "Where did you get these skills?"

Darcy squeezed Candy's foot and whispered, "I know what a woman needs."

Candy had no doubt in her mind about that.

Darcy moved to her other foot. At this point, Candy decided to go with it.

"What do you think they're talking about?" Candy asked Darcy, who seemed entranced by Candy's feet.

"Money. What else?" Darcy reached for her glass of champagne, holding both of Candy's legs. Darcy touched Candy's hair, then the side of her face. "You are so exquisite." She went to kiss Candy on the lips, but Candy moved her head slightly to the side.

She swung her legs off Darcy and planted a slow, generous kiss on her cheek.

Darcy's face turned red, and for the first time that night, Candy felt she saw the real Darcy, with all pretentions dropped. "Thank you," she said softly. "I haven't been kissed, anywhere, in ages."

Candy watched sadness wash over Darcy's face. Before she could say anything, she heard Xavier and Ben.

Their laughs got closer as they came back in the room.

"Ladies, you won't believe this, but Ben knows more about aged scotch than I do. That has never happened with anyone before," Xavier said. The scent of alcohol exuded from his skin. Ben wasn't too far off.

"My grandfather owns one of the largest distilleries in Scotland," said Ben. "You and Candy must check it out with us. Right, Darcy?"

"I have a feeling we will be hanging out for a while," Darcy said.

Two weeks later, Ben signed on in a financial partnership with the studio in support of Xavier's upcoming film. It was one of the biggest movie deals in Hollywood history.

16

———

Xavier's career took a new spin. *Vanity Fair*, *Variety*, *Hollywood Reporter* all announced his new partnership with Ben Woo and Panther Studios. If Xavier had already been busy, he was even busier now. Elena started working on the set, too. With Xavier's help, she made an easy transition to meet the needs of Nick and his team, who had nothing but good things to say about her. She was assigned to work on makeup for the extras, and that was enough to keep Elena busy.

"If you lasted here more than a week, that means that you are here to stay," Xavier said as he came inside one of the trailers she was working in to check on the crew.

"It's amazing," Elena said as she dabbed the last few bits of powder on an extra's face, a forty-nine-year-old cashier with freckles and the deepest dimples. She carefully put away her makeup tools to give Xavier her full attention and get ready for lunch with Michael. "I haven't felt this alive since my days working on the fashion shows. There's so much energy on these sets. This," Elena raised her arms, "should be bottled and sold."

Xavier watched her eyes light up talking about the place. It always seemed like an office to him, where work needed to be done. But listening to her gave it a fresh perspective. "Yeah, I mean. I can see it that way sometimes. Particularly, when things are going my way."

They both laughed.

Elena patted him on the shoulder. She rested her hand there. "Everything seems to go your way, Xavier. Really good work you are doing here. I couldn't think of a place better."

"Thank you," he said with a light laugh. "I should be easier on myself I guess."

"No, thank you," she said and landed a peck on his cheek. "I'm really thankful to you. And Candy."

"It was all her idea." He touched the side of his face she kissed, taken aback by it. "I'll let her know we spoke."

Just then, the trailer door opened.

Elena's eyes widened as she took in Michael. "Hey, baby," she said, almost forgetting her lunch with him. "Come in, meet Xavier."

"Hey, man, how are you?" Xavier held out his hand, which Michael reached for slowly.

"Hey, nice to meet you. Did I interrupt something?"

Xavier and Elena both looked at each other with their mouths open, not sure who would speak first. "No, of course not," Elena replied. "Xavier, was there anything else?"

"Nah, I just wanted you to know we're happy with you here. Keep up the good work," he said. "Pardon me." He slid in between them and left.

Elena put her arms around Michael's neck and pulled him close. "What do I owe this sexy surprise?"

As he looked down at her, Elena's eyes squinted in a sensual way.

"What is up with you and Xavier? You guys seemed really close."

Elena let go of his neck and took a few steps back. "You would have to say something stupid, wouldn't you?"

"'I don't know. Lately, you just seem . . . different. Like, this is more important to you than anything."

"Different or happier?" she asked, walking back up to him. "Aren't you happy to see me happy?"

"I'm happy," he said, not convincing Elena.

She grabbed her bag. "Okay, so are you here then to take me to lunch?"

"No," he said. "I had to pick Michaela up from school today. She threw up the breakfast I made. Now she won't eat anything until you come home."

"Michael..." Elena whined.

"What do I do?"

"I can't just leave now." She opened the trailer door, and they walked down the steps. The cool afternoon air and sun kissed her face.

"We supposed to wait until you get home at midnight like you been doing?" Michael raised his voice, as if being outside in front of others ignited him.

"Did you really come to complain about the kids? Or did you come for something more?" She got up in his face to keep the words close between them.

His eyes looked away from her. "I wanted to come to see what this was all about. What's got you so jazzed up."

"Ahh, checking up on me. So like you."

"You know, the hell with this! You want to sacrifice your kids and me. Go ahead," he shouted, waving his hand in front of her face.

She pressed her lips tightly, talking to him through her teeth. "Michael, you are causing a scene. And you're not a paid actor around here. You need to leave."

"Is everything all right?" asked Vince, a Samoan security guard who was part of the security crew on site. "Does he need to leave?"

"No, no. This is my husband. He was just leaving," Elena said, giving Michael the eye.

Michael turned around to see people staring in their direction. "I'm leaving. Yeah, right." He scowled at the guard. But Michael knew better.

"Give me another minute, Vince."

Vince walked away, but not too far.

"Michael, I worked hard all morning. If you are not taking me to lunch, I'm going to eat. And then I am coming back *here*. See you tonight."

She waited until he finally walked off and joined the crew outside having lunch under the tent.

17

———————

Candy had more time to herself now that Elena had a job. She spent most of her days attending charity brunches, reading, and exercising. The last was an investment she would always make in herself, and besides, she was obligated to it as per the contract to remain fit. She couldn't think of a better motivation to get on a treadmill. Xavier made sure he kept in touch with Candy throughout the day, maybe even too often. At one point, he was calling Candy every two hours, like Cleveland did in the beginning of their relationship.

Candy and Elena relaxed by the pool on one of Elena's days off. It was nearly eighty degrees on a sunny Sunday.

Candy poured tanning oil into her palm. "Sometimes Xavier mystifies me."

"What do you mean?" asked Elena.

"He treats me like his real wife. And in a way, I'm falling for him, I think." Candy rubbed the massage oil on her arms.

"You are falling in love?" Elena slipped down her shades in question.

"Hmph," Candy said, sitting up on the edge of her recliner. "Okay, not yet. But I wonder if I could. What if he and I are really right for each other?"

"Candy, you said yourself that was a major no-no." Elena waved her finger. "Then what happens to the contract?"

"We tear it up," Candy said, taking a deep breath.

"And part with all that money? That is not you."

"What's giving up a few millions when I can have all of this and all of him?" Candy said, opening her arms wide. "Xavier is going to make money for decades. Money is not the only reason. I like him. A lot."

"Are you doing this because Cleveland is now with Marlene? I know you never stopped loving him."

Candy ignored the knot in her throat hearing what Elena said and shrugged it off. "I've been thinking of my future a lot lately. I'm getting up there, and I want someone to love forever like everyone else."

"You're not available anyway, for long-term love," Elena teased. "You put too much into this."

"I am available," Candy snapped back. But she didn't know. Annoyed by the assumption, she walked to the edge of the pool and let the coolness of the water envelop her.

Elena jumped in behind her and swam around to face Candy.

"Girl, you are lucky. Look at all your man gives you. If you make it official, what happens to your payout? You lose money."

"That can be worked out," Candy corrected her. "Anyway, I was just talking hypothetically. Nothing is changing."

They both swam to the edge and relaxed against the side of the pool, watching the gold and red hues of the setting sun.

"Sometimes, I wonder if marriages would be better the way you do it. Where everyone knows what to do and where they stand. Where expectations are set early and there is an expiration date."

"Could you handle that?" Candy asked as she combed her fingers through her wet hair.

"Elena twisted her mouth. "It depends. I'd have to pick him, like you do."

Candy nodded slowly. "I've been lucky that I never wanted to walk out on a contract. Being married this way helps me feel more secure. I worry, though, that as I get older it will get harder to be a professional wife."

"As soon as things get hard, people give up," said Elena. "Don't give up, Candy."

"My life is based on fairy tales. You have no idea what I would have done for a real marriage years ago. Even though yours isn't perfect, it is real."

"Well, that is true," Elena agreed. "I guess nothing is ever perfect. All I can say is follow your heart. Wherever it goes." They rose out of the pool and walked back to their recliners, where fresh glasses of ice-cold mimosas waited.

At that moment, Xavier walked into the pool area with a glass of scotch in his hand. "What a beautiful sight," he said, sauntering toward them.

Both Candy and Elena had on string bikinis. Candy had to admit that Xavier wasn't lying. They looked good.

He walked over and gave Candy a kiss on her lips. The taste of chlorine was still on her mouth, but he didn't care. He ran his fingers down the sides of her body. "You taste delicious," he whispered.

Candy smiled.

He turned to Elena and took her hand. "Nick missed you on the set today. He says you're doing great work."

Elena's cheeks flushed red. "Thank you," she said, diverting her eyes back to Candy. "Everyone has been so welcoming."

"Well," Xavier said, "I see you ladies been enjoying your day."

Candy's phone rang. It was her bank. "Let me take this call really quick," she said, going inside the house.

"Elena, I do want to talk to you about the other day," Xavier said as they both stood poolside. "Are you okay?"

"Yes." Elena toweled her hair, uncomfortable about bringing up what happened. She thought maybe she should have been the first.

"I don't allow spouses on the set. I'm sorry if I didn't make that clear."

"I'm sorry, I didn't know. He just popped up. He's like that sometimes."

"It can't happen again," he said in a firm manner.

"Yes, definitely not." Elena watched as he walked back inside.

Candy joined Elena when she was done, and they went back to sipping until the sun fully set.

18

"Mrs. Oshun, would you like more cappuccino?" Greta asked, indicating Candy's empty cup.

"Yes, please." Candy held the cup up for a refill. "Greta, where did you learn to make these delicious cappuccinos? I've paid up to seven dollars for a good one, and this is by far better than any of them."

"*Italia*," Greta said, with her thick accent. "My grandmother always make it the best." She went back to cutting up the bits for another dish she made exceptionally well, Cobb salad.

Candy, wrapped in a silk kimono robe with nothing underneath, rested her slender yet curvy body on the stool at the kitchen island. She thumbed through the TV channels before reading a magazine on Kindle. It was a rainy Tuesday afternoon, and with Xavier gone and the house fairly quiet, Candy happily took the time to indulge in total relaxation.

She ordered a few new paintings for the living room. She was unofficially charged with changing them every other month, and she liked to focus on a new theme. Last month was Emergence, focusing on all things coming out of their shells or out of the dark. She then checked on her rental properties, sent her family a monthly check, deposited funds into the account that she opened for her sister's school fees, and paid a few other personal bills.

She picked up her cell phone to dial her sister. When she answered, Candy said, "Lettie, my love. I miss you."

Lettie's voice was soft and quiet. "You won't believe what happened this time."

As CANDY DROVE to her mom's house, she thought about all that had happened between them and why their relationship couldn't be normal. She felt she always had to jump in and save the day. What would they do without her? She knew Lettie would be fine, but her mother, a woman who couldn't stand the sight of her, needed her every dollar. She thought, was she any different?

Candy was terrified of being hurt and left alone with no one she could depend on. She lived as a fixer. Being a professional wife was a natural offshoot of what she already knew growing up. She learned to protect and take care of herself from a young age. Her mother would abandon her for weeks while she hunted down her dad and his women. Candy sighed as she turned up the music in her car, waiting in traffic.

She thought about how at age nine she put herself to bed, learned how to wash her face properly, tended to her period and everything that came in between. Candy was always embarrassed about her early development. A teacher, Ms. Baxter, had taught her about pads when she caught Candy with a red backside one afternoon in class.

The other students laughed so hard that Candy didn't leave her desk for the rest of the day, even during lunch. A part of Candy died that day because she literally felt like she was dying. She had no idea that the blood was normal. Ms. Baxter took her to the grocery store that afternoon and bought her a bag of twenty-two pads. The number of pads blew Candy's mind as a child.

"That should be good for the next few months," she said. "Make sure you go to the same store. Bring the empty bag. Show them. Tell them you want the *same* thing," Ms. Baxter said. She was a big brown woman with long, delicious hair that she braided in two thick plaits that fell down her back.

Ms. Baxter knew that Candy had a mother that didn't really care for her kids. Her mother cared only for her father and was always waiting on him. He didn't so much as call them.

Ms. Baxter taught Candy how to predict her period by looking at the moon. Candy loved that part. Her period would fall on a full moon like clockwork. She'd mark the full moon days on her calendar with happy faces.

A few months later, still nine years old, Candy followed Ms. Baxter's rules. She brought the empty bag to the store before the next full moon, with a few dollars from a candy sale, and the man behind the counter gave it to her. She had never felt more grown and in charge of herself.

Ms. Baxter warned her. "When you see a full moon and no blood, that means you need to tell an adult."

Inside, Candy knew what that meant, even though she didn't say it. She taught herself to be a woman from elementary school on out. She learned how to wash her face following the three-step process in every teen magazine. She read about the right moisturizers, how to shave her legs smooth, and which bras to wear with what outfits. Later, she became one of the most popular girls in high school, not because of how she looked but because of what she taught other girls.

Candy parked in front of the house and could immediately see the roof damage. It looked like a small part had caved in. She hadn't said she would be stopping by because her mother might refuse to open the door again. Lettie had let Candy know that they would be home all day.

As Candy walked up the porch steps, her mother gave her a stern look.

"Mommy," Candy said. "I heard about the leak in the roof."

"Hi," Ms. Robertson said, her tone curt. She stood up and called, "Lettie, your sister is here for you."

"Mommy, I'm here for you, too," Candy interrupted. "Not just Lettie."

Ms. Robertson cut her eyes at Candy. "You come over here without calling. You want your money back?"

"No, Mommy." Candy couldn't allow herself to get offended. Her mother was growing older. She had much more gray than last time, and the wrinkles were more deeply rooted around her eyes and jawline. "I'm here to see you."

Lettie burst out onto the porch, giving her sister a hug so big that it nearly knocked Candy off her feet.

Lettie turned to her mother, who had already walked inside the house. Walking beside Candy into the living room, she whispered, "I'm so glad you didn't call."

"Me, too," Candy whispered. "Is she coming back downstairs?"

"Probably not." Lettie frowned.

Candy smiled back at her, watching the stream of water from the living room ceiling fall into a bucket. "I'm going up to talk to Mommy," she said, hopping off the sofa.

She walked up the steps and followed the sound of a TV in the bedroom.

Candy stopped at the door. "Mommy, can I talk to you?"

Her mother didn't answer.

"Can I come in, please?" Candy asked again.

Candy opened the door, walked over, and sat at the edge of the bed. She looked around. Her mother had the latest flat-screen TV, nearly as big as the wall. She spotted the closet brimming with designer clothes, shoes, and bags. Labels still attached. "Mommy, what are you doing with all the money? The house is falling apart A leak like that doesn't start overnight."

Ms. Robertson snapped at her. "Taking care of me and Lettie. Something your father never did."

"Why don't you fix up this house?"

"Just because you bought this house doesn't mean you have a say in it. You and your sister are just dumb asses." The words rolled off Ms. Robertson's tongue, slow and deliberate.

That stung Candy.

"I got you the best cardiologist in the country. Are you taking your meds?"

Candy thought about the nearly three thousand dollars a month she spent on the meds, not including her mother's routine doctor visits.

"I am," Ms. Robertson said. "Anything else?"

"What about the house? I can hire people to help you keep it up. Make it look nice."

"Why? No one comes to see us anyway." Ms. Robertson lit a cigarette.

Candy winced. She hated the smell, and her mother knew that. "Anytime I come over, you wouldn't let me in Mommy. The question is, who are you keeping out?"

Ms. Robertson blew the smoke in Candy's face.

Candy coughed.

"Who are you to be asking people questions?" Ms. Robertson said. "The only way you can keep a man is if he buys you."

Candy felt like she had been punched in the stomach.

She hurried out of the room, her hand over her mouth. She ran down the steps. "I gotta go."

Before she could get to the door, she noticed Lettie waiting for her. "She really thinks you're a prostitute," Lettie said. "She's so stupid."

"Don't call her stupid, Lettie. She just doesn't understand what I do. I'm sure if she had the same opportunity I did, she would have taken it, too. So, forget all that. How are you? You need anything?"

"No. I'm okay. Going to school full-time has been good for me. And Max."

"Ohh." Candy cooed, feeling lifted by the pleasure her sister's smile exuded.

"We're spending more time together," Lettie said. "He is so kind. He studies a lot, so we give each other space."

"That's right you make sure you study too. Get that degree and be done." Candy said, hugging her by the shoulders. Her sister was going to graduate next year, and Candy was just as excited as she was.

"I'm here if you need anything," Candy reminded her.

"And I am here for *you*, too," Lettie said, walking Candy to the door.

19

When Candy's cell rang, she didn't recognize the number but answered anyway. "Hello?"

"Candy! This is Marlene. Do you have a minute?"

"Marlene?" Candy's tone was curt. A voice in her mind told her to hang up, but she was too curious to find out what Marlene wanted.

"Dear, I'm so sorry to alarm you. I was hoping we could meet. I feel we got off on the wrong foot when we met. Can we get together? At your convenience, of course."

"Marlene, we have no business together. What do we need to meet for?"

"Darling—"

"*Don't.*"

"Candy. I-I just want to talk to you about Cleveland. I want you to help me understand him."

"Does he know you are calling me?"

"Yes, this was his idea." Marlene mustered up strength in her voice. "It must be in person. You know I'm a face-to-face gal. I don't have the number-one talk show for nothing."

Candy bit her bottom lip as she thought. What could be happening between them? "I have time around two," she said.

"Starbucks on Madison? I'm actually just a few stop lights from there now."

"Okay," Candy said dryly. She held the phone in her hand long after Marlene had hung up. Then she jetted to her closet, pulled out a backless peach sundress and slipped on her gold sandals.

Grabbing the brush, she bent over and combed out her bed hair until it was full of body and bounce again. She slipped a light gloss onto her lips, then donned dark shades and texted the driver to pull the car around.

WHEN MARLENE WALKED INTO STARBUCKS, the room seemed to shrink around her. Marlene was over six feet tall. She had glowing olive skin from her Italian and Black heritage and a reddish, pixie-cut wig. Her hips swayed so much as she walked that she nearly toppled the displays in her path. Candy sat at a window seat in the back, sipping chai tea latte and watching the crowd spin around to catch a glimpse of the daytime superstar, without an entourage.

Candy chuckled as Marlene stopped in the center of the room, her head swiveling about in an effort to spot her prey. Marlene dug in her bag for her cell phone. Candy let hers ring and let Marlene sweat it out a bit as a small crowd gathered around her for photos. Candy kept studying Marlene as she huffed her way through. There were actually small beads of sweat forming on her forehead.

"Marlene," Candy said, waving. She finally felt the need to release her from her suffering.

Marlene threw up her hand and marched toward her table. The crowd dissipated.

"Oh my, what was I thinking? Starbucks on Madison," Marlene said, collapsing onto the chair like a ton of bricks.

"I thought you'd have your people with you," Candy said, nursing her cup of chai.

Marlene leaned in, breathless. "I act like I hate it, but I love it."

"The attention?"

"Yes, I'm an actor first," Marlene said as she slipped her large Birkin bag off her arm and plunked it on the seat next to her. "The civilians need to see me living a normal life, too. My photos will be one of the most viewed on Instagram all day."

Candy should have known Marlene would pick a place where she could rub her celebrity in her face. This was when Candy appreciated her under-the-radar, hidden-in-plain-sight life.

Candy put her cup down. "Why are we here, Marlene?"

"Darling—oh, sorry," Marlene said, playfully touching her lips. "*Candy*. Can I get you anything else?"

"No, I'm fine—"

"I was hoping that we could talk."

"Well, for a number-one talk show host, you're not very good at it," Candy said.

Marlene's smile began to wither. She batted her thick, too-large glued-on eyelashes. "Cleveland is still in love with you."

Candy looked on, expressionless. It would take a whole lot more to drop her guard around Marlene.

"What did you do? How did you do it? I can't even get him to have sex with me after three months," Marlene pleaded.

Candy didn't flinch.

"He always compares me to you. Why can't I dress like you? Talk like you. Even make love like you. He is so cruel."

Candy reached for her cup and took a slow, long swig.

"But you know what he does instead of being a good husband? He goes off to St. Barth's and finds some hussy in the sand, and—"

Candy put her hand up. "Enough. If you're trying to get me on your side for some tirade you're planning against Cleveland, forget it. What else is happening with you guys?"

Marlene's eyes zoomed in on Candy. "He likes me to stay clothed, while he is naked. I feel so awkward. It's some weird fetish thing he has, right?"

Candy listened as Marlene carried on, but what she said didn't sound like Cleveland at all.

"And I'm learning," Marlene went on. "Oh, he has no idea what he started. If he only knew how much I know now, he may never get out of bed," she said with a sly smile, looking for a reaction from Candy.

Candy took a deep breath, trying to figure out Marlene's angle. "Cleveland is no different than any other man. They get tired and bored. I really can't help." She pushed her empty cup to the side. "Maybe it's a blessing in disguise that he's indifferent right now."

"For who?" Marlene said, sitting back in the chair.

Candy wondered if Cleveland told Marlene about their contract. He would never, she thought. No one could ever know.

Then Marlene started up again. "I tried everything I could think of. Blindfold, toys, dominatrix, you name it. He did tell me you were pretty good with all that. Especially *role playing*."

"Stop." Candy laughed a little, relieved that this direction was a lot better than what she thought. Still, her insides stewed about the stuff he did tell Marlene. Candy grabbed her bag. "I have another appointment to catch. Sorry."

"Candy," Marlene said. Her voice was stern, a bit louder than before. "It's not a good idea to blow me off."

Candy lifted her chin and flashed her eyes at Marlene.

Marlene lowered her voice. "Why don't you let me be your friend? You can feed some tips on Xavier, and I can make you look like a goddess on my show. Your PR cred will shoot through the roof."

Candy stood up. "You have nothing I need."

"I have everything you need," Marlene said, her lips turned down in disdain. "Like your name."

Candy turned around and walked out of Starbucks, all the while cursing Cleveland for marrying a big mouth like Marlene. She deemed it time to visit him to make him shut up. Candy's whole future was now at the mercy of Marlene's sticky fingers.

20

———

"**E**lena, you are not a makeup artist but a magician," said Juan, another makeup artist, after she finished making a fifty-year-old extra look twenty years younger. That was her fifteenth extra in just under three hours.

She hadn't sat down in all that time, but she wasn't tired. She pulled a cleaning wipe from her makeup station and wiped off the makeup dust and stains on the counter, oblivious to the fact that they had an assistant who would do that. Her station was the neatest of all the makeup artists, and as she wiped it to a spotless gleam, she admired it. Why did other makeup artists litter their stations with makeup bottles or used tissues? She took a few extra minutes and ran a broom through the entire makeup trailer. A few of the artists thanked her as she cleaned up around their stations, too. "You're welcome." She smiled back, glad to be helping in any way she could.

"I need Alex on set now!" yelled an AD as he pushed his way into the trailer, tracking sandy dust from his boots. Alex, one of the secondary actors in the movie, hurried after the assistant director as they both ran out of the trailer with a makeup artist trailing behind. Elena quickly swept that mess up, too. As she swept, her stomach growled. She hadn't eaten anything in hours.

Xavier's movie set was a constant hive of activity, with equipment, people, and even animals shuttling back and forth like a circus. Stunt people practicing a scene in one area, a shootout happening in another. Elena felt like she was living her dream every day. In the mornings, she woke up with an extra bounce. She prepared the kids for school and for their school bus pickup. Michael slept till noon most days, even weekends. His sloth didn't bother her anymore as her new gig made her feel hopeful again. Thanks to Candy. How could she pay her back? She had given her not only a job but her self-esteem again. She thought about taking her out to lunch for starters.

"Thanks, Elena, Great job today," Nick, the head makeup artist, said as he flew by on his way to one of the A-list celeb trailers. Elena watched, wondering if she could ever get to that level.

It was around noon as she washed her brushes and prepped her station for the next round later that afternoon. She looked out her trailer window, watching Xavier order everyone around.

"No, I need that set up in thirty minutes, or you're not going home," he said, waving his arms at another man, who nodded patiently. "Now, you only have twenty-nine!" She admired his take-charge manner and didn't understand why he was called a bully or a nightmare.

"Camille!" he yelled over the intercom to an actress who was known as the diva on set, but Xavier didn't care. "Get your ass to Lot Ten now. Five, four, three ..."

"Take-charge" described all the men in her strong Romanian family of mostly women. They went toe for toe with each other, and nobody backed down. She thanked them for showing her what strength really looked like. She couldn't figure out how she ended up with Michael. He was so weak and indecisive. She wondered what would have come of her if she chose better.

A half hour later, she heard a knock on her trailer. She put down the cup of granola yogurt she bought from home, as a buffer against using the fattening craft service. She checked the time, and it was still too early for anyone. A bit frustrated, she repeated Nick's mantra to herself. *The point is to get the makeup done on time, not too early, so it stays fresh for the shoot under the hot L.A. sun.* But she didn't feel confident enough to turn anyone down. She wiped her hands and opened the door.

"Wanna grab some lunch?" Xavier said, standing there with a pad in his hand. His assistant, Paul Rexter, a short, red-haired man in his twenties, stood behind him, holding a notepad. They both looked at her, waiting for an answer.

"Sure!" Elena yelped, embarrassed at her eagerness. *Xavier Oshun and his assistant want to have lunch with me?* She hoped that meant good news for her future. Elena grabbed her handbag and followed them to the parking lot. Xavier's cell rang, and he excused himself. He called Paul over and gave him the phone. Then he walked back to Elena.

"Sorry, I have to attend to something really quick—"

"Xavier, man, don't worry, I got it covered," Paul said, waving. "I'll catch up with you guys later."

Elena was relieved. She was glad to be left alone with Xavier, to get to know him and the business better.

"Are you okay with it just being the two of us?" Xavier asked as they both walked to a small café a block away.

"Yes, of course," Elena said. "I can ask you all the stupid questions I have without being embarrassed." Wisps of the cool breeze ran up her arms, and she regretted not bringing her sweater.

"Embarrassed? I wanted to have this lunch to see if you had any questions. How are you coming along?"

Elena turned to him. "Does Candy know we're going out for lunch together?"

"This whole thing was her idea. She thought it would be good for me to sit down with you. Make sure you're okay so far. Folks around here can smile in your face and stab you in the back."

"Right," she said, a bit disappointed that the lunch wasn't a spontaneous idea of his. Her body warmed up with every step she took. A sweater would have ruined her outfit anyway, she thought.

They arrived at the café, and he ordered for both of them. He ordered the choice she had made last time. His memory impressed her, but she didn't want to make a big deal out of it. He handed her the frothy frappe and chef salad, and collected his food.

"Is there anything else you need, Mr. Oshun?" the white-haired woman behind the counter asked, smiling warmly at him.

"Thanks, Claudette," he said.

Elena wiped her bangs away from her eyes to get a good look at the woman, who seemed so happy that he was patronizing their store. "Do you come here a lot?"

"I try to support the local businesses. Candy thinks that's important. Looks good."

A small fireplace kept the café comfortable and cozy, with soft jazz music in the background. Christmas lights had been hung up above, gleaming down on the steaming cups of lattes and plates of pastries. They sat by a window and talked about how the day was going, and how Elena's first month on the set had come and gone. She told Xavier how kind everyone had been to her and how she felt like she fit right in.

"They also know I brought you in," he said with a warning in his tone. "Don't get too close for comfort. They'll use you to get to me."

"Oh," Elena said, wondering why she had never had this conversation with Candy, who was light-years savvier about these things than she was. "I would never share your private life details."

"Well," he said, after he chewed a bite of his roast beef sandwich. "What goes without question is your exceptional talent. Now, to have you on this or any more sets, you do need to be credentialed," he said, explaining to her where to do that. "That way people will take you seriously when you work elsewhere. Nick can help you."

Elena lightly chewed her salad, savoring the bits of eggs and ham. "No problem. But what if I didn't want to work elsewhere? I really like working with *you*. I feel comfortable."

Their eyes met in the silence that followed.

"What I mean is that I want to build my experience. But I want to work more with you, on your sets, as I get more skills under my belt."

Xavier's eyes sparkled. "That's fine. But if I'm not working, you're not working. So that's what I mean. To keep working you need to be credentialed."

Elena nodded. A few other people from the set walked in and placed their orders. The opening door let in a breeze that energized the fire, warming the place again. Clouds rolled in like rain was nearby. As they finished their meals, Elena said, "I want to learn as much about the business as possible. Not just makeup. I want to learn everything. From you."

Xavier nodded his head. "What if you joined Candy and me at a gala in a few weeks? I know it is short notice, but some important people will be there. You can borrow a dress from wardrobe if you need something. There'll be people at the party you should meet."

Elena bit her lip like someone had just presented a delicious plate of her favorite chocolate fudge. "Thank you."

LATER THAT AFTERNOON, she took Xavier up on his offer. With Izzy, a Thai ladyboy who was one of the best costume designers in the industry, she combed through the vintage costumes of the eighteenth century, dresses that looked straight off the runway. Her arms grew sore from trying on a dozen dresses. After an hour, she landed on the perfect size six dress that accentuated her full, freckled breasts and tiny waist. The deep sage green contrasted with her smooth, flawless pearl-colored skin. Izzy also helped her find a pair of heels, which only took a few minutes.

"These are gonna kill it." Izzy held up a pair of vintage Chanel sling backs with a nearly five-inch heel.

Elena's feet slid into the heels like nothing. "I don't have anything at home close to these."

"Mere mortals aren't supposed to."

Elena beamed at the entire ensemble together, and Izzy packed it away for her. *I have to thank Xavier before I leave.* After she thanked Izzy, she made her way to Xavier's trailer. The afternoon rain, which forced the set to close early, left a cool mist behind, eased by the setting afternoon sun. But Xavier and a few others were still around. Right before she reached his trailer, Candy walked out glowing and took his hand.

Elena decided to leave it alone. She turned around and made a mental note to thank him tomorrow.

21

While mere mortals congregated on other side of town, Michael found himself in a pickle.

"I'm hurt, Daddy. I'm hurt!" His daughter came flying into the kitchen as he multitasked, washing the dishes and cleaning up before the kids' bedtime.

"Honey," he said as his daughter slammed into his thigh. He bent down and grabbed her shoulders. "Show me. What happened?"

Michaela sobbed uncontrollably, rubbing her eyes with both hands so that he could barely see her face. He pulled her hands down.

"Baby, what happened? I don't see anything wrong."

He turned her around and saw it. A big wad of red wetness.

"Did you fall?" he asked, embarrassed and confused at the same time. His daughter wasn't even developed, so the obvious answer was furthest from his mind.

His daughter kept crying uncontrollably, and Michael was just an inch away from crying himself, frantic that he couldn't help his child. He dialed Elena, but got no answer. Instead, he reached for the next best thing.

"Ahh, Candy, I need your help. Now. Please."

"Michael, is Elena okay?"

"No, I mean, yes. It's Michaela. She's bloody on her backside, down below, and she won't tell me why. Not sure if it is something she ate. Her face is flushed as well."

"Can you put her on the phone? It's her period."

Michael, as he handed over the phone, couldn't believe it. Neither could Michaela. He was relieved that Candy could help him figure out how to handle this.

"Honey, it's your period," Candy told her. "Did Mommy tell you anything about this coming now?"

"Who's coming?"

"Your period."

Michaela looked from side to side. "No, I don't think so. I mean, girls have it. But she said it wasn't time."

Michael ran upstairs and got her a fresh change of clothes but still wasn't sure what to do first.

Not long after, Candy came through the door. She saw dishes piled everywhere, dust bunnies dotting the carpets, and a smell of burnt grease permeated the air. "Michael? It's me." She stepped over a pile of clothes and rushed into the kitchen.

Michael and Michaela were waiting for her. He stood by while Candy took over.

"Michaela, I bought you some pads to help you. You are growing up to be a big girl. You just got your period."

"So, I do have my period?" Michaela breathed more slowly and took the bag from Candy, opening it. She opened a bag and smiled. "And they are pink. I love pink."

Candy gave Michael a beaming smile, who looked comforted, too. He was an old-fashioned Romanian guy. Candy understood his total helplessness.

"Why don't you take a quick shower and put on fresh clothes? Do you want me to show you how to wear these?"

She nodded.

Candy took Michaela upstairs and showed her how to put on a

pad, using one of the dolls in her room. Then Michaela took a shower, put on the pad, and slipped into a pretty purple pajama set.

"And this is for you, too." Candy placed a crown on Michaela's head, one she found at the toy aisle at the CVS before she came.

"Congratulations, baby," she said, giving her a hug. "How do you feel?"

"Happy," she said, crawling into her bed and flicking on the television.

"Okay, remember. You may have to change these in the morning or in the night time. So, if you get up to use the bathroom, look at it to see if you need a new one."

"What if it falls off?"

"It won't."

"Why didn't Mommy come home tonight?"

Candy touched Michaela's arm, feeling her deep loss of her mom in this moment. "Honey, she's working hard. I know your mommy wants to be here."

Michaela nodded, pulling her knees to her chest. Then Michael Jr. walked in. He had heard and seen everything.

"Hey, honey bun," Candy said, waving for him to join them.

"Is Michaela okay?" he asked Candy, his eyes wet with what looked like tears.

"Yes, of course, baby. Just girl stuff. Mommy will talk to you guys."

"I miss Mommy," Michael Jr. said, rocking his small body back and forth.

"I wish she wasn't working so hard. Everything is so different now. Even me," Michaela said, her eyebrows coming together.

No child likes change, Candy thought. She wanted to tell them nothing had changed. But she'd be lying. It pained her to see them miss their mother, especially on these kinds of days when things didn't go as planned.

Michaela grabbed Candy and gave her a deep hug. "Thank you. Ms. Candy."

Candy hugged the two children and left them alone. She found Michael waiting at the bottom of the steps.

"How is she?"

"She'll survive." Candy flashed a smile. "Let's just say, Elena and her will have a lot to talk about. She may need to explain to Michael, too, since he saw it all." Candy headed to the door.

"Wait, can I get you something to drink? Water?" he asked, already pulling out a glass.

"Okay," Candy said hesitantly, seeing Michael's energy boost at her agreeing to stay.

"Thank you again for tonight—and helping Elena get back to work."

"Sure. I'd do anything for Elena."

"I feel like she has changed since taking the job."

"Me, too. Definitely a happier woman."

"Yes, but it's like she doesn't need me anymore. Have you noticed anything?"

Candy paused while she finished her water. "I noticed that she has more energy. She seems more free-spirited, engaged."

Michael leaned against the kitchen counter. "There's more. I can't put my finger on it. Even tonight, she could have at least called us back. And she used to always pick up her phone."

Candy raised her chin slightly at where this was going. "Maybe you need to talk with her. The set is a busy place. Lots of noise. She might not have heard the phone." But Candy knew Elena's phone stayed glued to her, particularly because of her YouTube channel and the tons of messages she received.

"I will," he said, sounding disappointed at no big reveal from Candy.

Candy wondered if she was missing something, too.

22

———————

Dinners, receptions, brunches, and galas took up Candy's calendar for the next few weeks. Xavier's visibility had boomed, and studios and actors vied for the chance to work with him. He began to buckle under the pressure to perform. He started drinking an extra glass or two at their outings, which worried Candy. Xavier had to remain under control. If she took her focus off him too long, he would wander back into tabloid hell.

Tonight, was no different. In a few hours, they would be special guests at a gala for Bright Hope, a charity for foster children. She had been donating regularly to Bright Hope, creating a special trust fueled by Xavier's movie assets. She had proposed the idea one day with him at dinner, and he loved it. Xavier's movies were iconic, and she expected it to help build Bright Hope for decades. After they married, Candy took over Xavier's position on the charity's board, and she had become the number one fundraiser. She absolutely loved raising money. She knew what people needed to hear to act upon their belief in worthy causes. In fact, making people feel the best they could while they gave the best they could was her strong suit.

In the car on the way to the gala, Xavier planted a kiss on Candy's naked shoulder. "Have I told you how delicious you look tonight?" He grazed his lips across her neck. "Have I thanked you for all you're doing for me?"

"You have," Candy said, running her hand along his freshly shaven face. Their tongues touched as Xavier leaned his hard body toward hers.

Candy held back. "We don't want to go in there smelling all musty." She adjusted the bodice of her black ball gown. "Though I would like to see you get through all of this armor I got on," she said, pointing at the elaborate fabric and intricate design of her dress.

Xavier grinned and reached for a bottle of Cîroc from the backseat bar. "I gotta take the edge off somehow," he murmured. He poured himself a shot. "Want some?"

"Xavier," Candy hissed as he downed it and poured himself a second shot. "Can you at least wait till after the dinner?"

Just as he was about to go for a third one, Candy took his wrist and grabbed the bottle from his hand. "We need to discuss this at some point. You've got to get yourself together. You need a better way of handling the pressure."

Xavier fixed his mouth to say something, but in the end, he didn't. He put the cup away and settled into his seat. They drove to the dinner in silence.

CANDY MINGLED with a few of the other wives at the bar. The gala turned out to be another who's-who event with Xavier busier than ever. At one point, he found himself talking to Rick Blatt, an Oscar–winning actor, and a few seconds later, he was chatting with an important financier. Xavier moved from one person to the other with lightning speed. He hadn't had a single drink since the car ride, as far as she knew.

Candy noticed him talking to Ben and another gentleman named Maxwell Crew, whose wife, Isabel, Candy had met and befriended on the charity board.

Isabel was a petite, slender Argentinean woman in her late twenties with black hair and dark eyes. She was one of the few wives Candy knew who didn't opt for blonde tresses or extensions. But Isabel and Candy were from two different worlds. Maxwell was a major financier and connector, and Isabel was a former lawyer.

"Don't you feel sorry for our men? The way their work is never done," Isabel cooed playfully as she watched them in their small groups.

"As long as it keeps them out of the house, I'm not mad," said another wife named Deidra Sparks, whom Candy knew though not personally. Deidre was a thirty-five-year-old former stripper with extra pounds and a curly blonde wig who had lucked out by connecting with seventy-five-year-old Forest Graham, a studio head. Rumor was that Deidre wasn't all female. People said there was no way to really know, but Candy wasn't so sure about that.

That's an Adam's apple if I ever saw one, she thought.

"How do you keep yourself busy when Xavier's never home, Candy?" Deidra queried. "If he's anything like my man, you are lucky if you see him at all."

The women moved in closer.

"So, who are you slippin' and slidin' with?" Deidra asked, smiling.

They all laughed as if the question was an inside joke. Candy knew they all had lovers.

"Xavier, of course," she said.

"Ahh, you need to find yourself a snuggle boo," Isabel said. "Our men are not nearly as interested in us as they are in each other."

This surprised Candy. She hadn't expected that from Isabel. Candy thought this new Hollywood world was still unraveling its secrets for her.

"I have my own interests," Candy replied. "Mostly working out. I volunteer, do some charity work..."

Candy noticed as each lady's wide eyes began to fade.

"Do you think we're all here for a stupid charity? You and Isabel can bust your asses on charity boards, but all I have to do is write a check to get into a place like this. That's all it is. The filet mignon, the schmoozing, the photos," Deidra said.

Candy and Isabel rolled their eyes at each other. But deep inside, Candy respected the honesty. She had created this life to avoid toiling at a nine-to-five job herself. But purpose still mattered to her. Each man she married gave her an unbelievable chance to serve others through their philanthropy.

"Ladies, excuse me," Candy said, slipping away.

She spotted Xavier in an animated exchange with another man she couldn't identify. She walked in their direction.

Suddenly, she heard her name from behind her.

"Candy."

It was Elena, looking striking in a hunter green and black gown with a mermaid bottom that accentuated her curves and skin tone. Her hair was loosened on her shoulders in a tumble of shiny black waves. What Michael said about her changing made all the sense to her now.

She stopped dead in her tracks. Elena was the last person she expected to see tonight. She felt excitement and surprise at the same time.

"Hey, honey," she said as they embraced. What brings you here?" Candy tried to sound excited, but wish she would have told her she was coming.

Elena half-smiled, shifting her gown a bit as if she didn't know what to do with her hands. "Xavier invited me. He wanted it to be a surprise for you."

"For me? Wow, I've invited you before, and you never come." Candy felt a pain in her chest, as though something didn't feel right, like the scene at Elena's house she had to save the other night.

"Xavier thought it would be good for me to meet people to further my career."

Candy looked at Elena intently. She hadn't mentioned the incident with her daughter at the house. And Candy didn't want to make her friend feel any guiltier than any other working mom would. She let it go and finally managed a smile. "Okay, so let's introduce you to some folks." She bent her arm for Elena to put her arm through it.

She bought her around to a few people that she had mingled with earlier. When she felt that Elena was doing well enough on her own, she took a trip to the bar. She sipped, watching as Xavier and Elena made their separate rounds. She thought about the change she saw in Elena's family. They could never compete with these types of events in Elena's new world.

A few minutes later, Elena sauntered over with a playful look on her face. "You won't believe who is here."

Candy put her drink down and looked in the direction of where Elena was pointing. It was Cleveland. This time, the sight of him pleased her.

Elena waved him over. "I'll leave you two alone," she said and walked away.

Before Candy could respond, Cleveland was striding toward her. "You can't tell me you love him," he said, stopping right in front of her.

Cleveland looked dashing in a perfect black Armani tuxedo and cuff links. He towered over her. "So nice to see you again," she said, locked in his gaze. She took a deep breath and didn't let it go. It was like the whole room had stopped. Whatever happened between them last time was old news to her. She was glad to see him.

After Cleveland obtained drinks for them, he took her hand and escorted her away from the bar. Candy glanced around the room. Elena and Xavier were chatting, and she figured Elena was probably keeping him busy so he wouldn't focus on her with Cleveland. She spotted Marlene, who had come in at the cocktail hour with a slew of other guests.

Her gaze collided with Marlene's icy stare. Candy played it cool and turned her attention back to Cleveland, taking him in completely. His cologne smelled like sandalwood, and gray specks of hair speckled his beard like tiny diamonds. They talked, catching up on the latest news of Cleveland's business as well as his ailing grandmother, for whom he had arranged for twenty-four-hour care.

Same old Cleveland, Candy thought as she listened to him. He, of course, left out some important details.

Marlene sat perched at a table nearby, surrounded by her hangers-on, glancing at Candy every chance she got.

"I met up with Marlene. She called me up asking about advice in bed."

He narrowed his eyes. "She spoke to you?"

"Yes," Candy said, annoyed, but at this point not too much. "Why are you talking about me with her?"

"I'm not talking about you exactly," Cleveland insisted. "We got into an argument, and I told her that's why some men hire wives. Something like that."

Candy clenched her teeth. "How could you marry a big-mouthed talk show host?" She talked through her teeth, keeping her words low and minced. "I know she didn't want to talk about sex. She was just digging for dirt on me, you, anything."

Cleveland lowered his voice, too. "I fucked up, Candy, when you married Xavier—"

"Don't blame your decisions on me."

"Believe me, she won't bother you again. There's too much at stake for both of us. My reputation and—"

"Well, you made your bed," Candy said, swirling her glass.

"You of all people should know how I feel about you," he said matter-of-factly.

Candy retreated an inch. She knew Cleveland was the type who would full-out kiss her in front of these people if she let him.

Candy took a sip of her drink as Cleveland walked away. She watched as the room started to thin and people left. Elena came over and said her goodbyes. Candy wondered about Elena staying out so late with what Michael had told her. It was well after midnight. She wanted to go home herself. After nearly four hours at this gala, she was spent. The night was slowing down with the once-jammed dance floor now nearly empty. She finally spotted Xavier, sitting alone and staring at his cell phone as if he'd had his fill of the night, too. She walked over.

"Hey you, everything okay?" she asked. She sat down beside him at a table covered with empty glasses of champagne, half-eaten plates, and other bites.

Vodka seeped from his breath. "What's with you and that guy?"

"Who?"

"I saw him talk to you before and tonight. You have some unfinished business with him?"

"Oh, Cleveland." Candy's brain felt foggy, but she wasn't going to start lying now. "He's one of my former clients."

Xavier cut a look at her. He knew what that meant. "I don't like it."

"Next time, I'll introduce you. That was rude of me. I didn't want to interrupt the work you had to do tonight." He still looked pissed, and she offered something further. "Cleveland's office handles all my matters."

"Right," Xavier said, looking suspicious. "You guys seemed pretty close."

And he was right, she thought. She liked being close to Cleveland, and no one in hell was going to change that.

23

Elena arrived home after three o'clock from the gala. It had ended hours ago. Without shame, she was one of the last people to leave, and she sat in the hotel lobby to chat with the remnants. She didn't want to go home to her life ever again. She loved her children and her husband, but they couldn't fill the holes she had. Tonight, filled her up with its overflow of ideas and energy. She had typically turned down these invites from Candy, who would always steal the show. She never felt seen when Candy was in the room, but tonight was different. She also didn't feel her immense shyness. She had things to talk about, and she was genuinely interested in what others had to say. She met several contacts who could be good follow-ups for more work or maybe something more.

Something awakened in Elena tonight that she hadn't felt in years. All night she mingled, even as she watched people gravitate toward Candy like the sun. *That should be me.* Elena flinched at her own words. With her looks and her body, she couldn't explain why she was off the mark. While she and Xavier hustled around the room with their own separate agendas, he did introduce her to some folks, as he promised. Coming home, she felt off kilter, stuck in a life when she wished for so much more than what she had.

She took a deep breath, slipped off her heels, and turned the lock to her front door. She walked in quietly and set her shoes by the door. She turned on a light in the hallway that led to the kitchen. The décor she took pride in—from her purple kitchen hand towels she bought from her last trip to Romania down to the lava lamp and houseplants—looked cheap and diminished after tonight. Frowning as she canvassed her home, she was disgusted that not one thing meant anything to her, even the living room sofa handed down by a relative. There was nothing of value, nothing with her story, her style, her needs.

She poured herself another drink. Her mind felt battered with thoughts of Xavier and Candy. It was like something was in the air tonight, she had sniffed too much and couldn't get it out. She unzipped the back of her dress and poured herself some more. Her chest heaved up and down as her body overheated, sweat gathered under her pits, and her breath tightened. She hadn't had a panic attack in years. She chugged another shot. After a few minutes, her shoulders relaxed.

"Really?" Michael said in Romanian, standing against the kitchen door. "You don't even call. It's after three a.m."

"Michael, I can't right now—"

"Can't do what?" he asked, charging toward her. "Ever since you got that job, you think you're one of them now. Don't you?"

Elena didn't answer.

"Ever since you started, you're not you no more. You dress differently. Smell differently. Talk differently." He took a deep breath. "The kids are awake. They didn't go to sleep because they were waiting for you."

"Tell them to go to bed," Elena said, sighing loudly. "Do you want me to put them to bed, too?"

"What do you think? You're their mother."

"Michael. I can't do this. We have to talk about a better way. I need a break."

"You think you can do better?"

"What's wrong with being better. . . feeling better?" she stammered.

"I spoke to Candy about you."

Elena straightened herself up. "Candy? When?" She slid the empty glass away from her.

"She came over and talked to the kids."

"What for?"

"I called her when Michaela got her period. *She* helped us."

Elena took the empty glass and poured herself another. She wiped her lips with the back of her hand. "You said you took care of everything that night."

"The kids needed their mother. But another woman had to step in. Make things right again," he said with a smirk. "You are going to lose everything if you keep this up."

Elena threw the rest of the drink in his face. He didn't flinch.

"Is that how you get me to be a better mother, a better wife? Go to hell. Everybody can go to hell!" She started toward the couch but stumbled.

Michael helped her up.

"Get the hell away from me. All of you. I want out of this mess."

"So just like that? We are nothing to you. What about the kids?"

"Why don't you and Candy figure out what to do this time?"

THE NEXT DAY, a day off for her, Michael left the house early, and while the kids were at school, Elena had the place to herself to gather her thoughts. She faintly remembered what she said just a few hours ago, but it felt like days ago. Her gut told her something bad happened last night.

Elena jumped at the ringing of her cell but answered quickly. "Hey, lady," Elena said when she heard Candy's voice. "You looked exquisite last night. I really hope you didn't mind I came."

"No way. I'm glad you made it. Xavier thought it was fine, and so did I. And excuse me, you were the bomb last night in that number. Elena, you had heads turning!"

Elena blushed. "I guess I did. I had to look right, so the wardrobe department helped me. Xavier was kind of enough to let me use something."

"They have the best clothes. I may have to get me a thing or two." She laughed. So did Elena. "Why do you sound down with everything that happened last night? Did you meet anyone?"

"I did. I met a few executives, plus another costume designer who said they want to work with me. You know, I've been thinking that I could do more than makeup. So I am open to learning. I told this to Xavier. I want to learn everything I can."

"Okay, I see you are getting your wings now. I knew you had it in you. So what's next?"

"Did Michael ask you to come by the other day to help with Michaela?"

"Yes, he did. I thought you knew."

"I didn't until I got home last night. What exactly happened?"

Candy thought for a moment. "Michaela got her period, and I bought her pads. Michael didn't know what to do. Typical man response."

"I see, well," Elena's good angel wanted to thank Candy, but her bad angel resented her for butting in. "Why didn't you just tell him what to do over the phone?"

"He asked me to come by. The way he sounded, I got a little worried."

Elena took a deep, long sigh.

"Is there something wrong?"

"You didn't tell me. He didn't tell me. I found out in this big explosion last night. Like he got some information from you. What did he say exactly?"

"He asked me if you changed."

"And you said?"

"No, but—"

"But what?"

"I said no that night. But you have changed, Elena."

Elena's chest stiffened. "Oh, so now you and Michael both think I'm a bad mom."

"Elena, if that is how you feel, that's how you feel. I never called you a bad mom. Neither did Michael to me. But you should have called back that night."

Elena struggled with taking a few breaths. "I know how uncomfortable it may have been for you to step in. So, thanks," she said in a dry manner.

There were a few moments of silence. Then she asked, "And Cleveland, were you happy to see him?"

The question seemed to catch Candy off guard. "I was, and I am. But I have my priorities. Namely, Xavier."

Elena pursed her lips. "You guys only have like three or four months left, right?"

Candy paused in her answer. "I think so. I stopped counting, really."

Elena noted the number in her head.

"Don't worry, Elena. When or if Xavier and I call it off, you will still have a job. I'll make sure of it."

"Yeah, yeah, no worries at all. I wasn't even thinking about that. So anyway, I want to thank you for being such a good friend. I hardly ever get to do anything nice for you. What about lunch on me? You pick the place."

"Okay, that sounds good," Candy sounded hesitant, "but you don't have to thank me. You have the talent and skills to do anything you want. Without me."

And Elena believed that. She had changed. Just like Candy said. And she was going to show Candy exactly how.

24

Wednesday morning, Candy found herself in the Tracy Anderson studio, getting a much-deserved workout to relieve her stress. She hadn't been feeling like herself lately. She had expected this marriage to be easier. She had expected it to be in and out. Lavish dinners and parties and then on to the next.

But this time, it had been flooded with the unexpected. Cleveland, Marlene—and Elena. She had never let a friend as close to her professional life as Elena, and she did not expect to get her a job with one of her clients. Elena had been around her clients before without issue, but a job was something else.

As she joined in on the cool-down exercises, she noticed a woman walk in late. She hadn't seen Darcy, Ben's wife, in months. From the back of the room, she had full view of Darcy's new butt. It was higher and thicker than she remembered. What Darcy failed to do, Candy thought, was to get the hips to go with it.

As the women in the studio said their goodbyes and exchanged promises of brunches and lunches, Candy stayed back. Before long, Darcy emerged from the group.

"Stranger," Candy said as she tapped Darcy. "Where've you been?"

Darcy tried to smile. Her new, enhanced lips refused to cooperate. She hugged Candy instead.

"I had to leave that fuck head. He's a narcissistic sociopath."

"Isn't that an oxymoron?" Candy said, fascinated that Darcy was seething with each word.

"I found him with another man."

"And that's a surprise?"

"No—"

"You knew he was gay," Candy pointed out.

"Yes, but we promised that if he slept with men, I'd get to be in on it, too. And I wasn't."

Candy nodded, doing her best to follow.

"And, unprotected."

"And how'd you know that?"

"I busted them in the act," Darcy, said clenching her fists. "I was so livid I attacked both of them."

"I see." Candy felt bad for Darcy, who she didn't realize until that night at the house how lonely she was. She thought Darcy's reaction was hilarious; she was less angry at being cheated on and more at not getting a cut.

"It's over," Darcy said. "I've had enough of all of this. And," she said, giving Candy a look-over, "I'm surprised you haven't."

"Oh?" Candy said, looking at Darcy side-eyed.

Darcy pulled Candy to a discreet corner. "Ben and Xavier are spending lots of time together. You know Ben's *office* is at Harriman Lake, and he has a house there. And we all know what that means around here."

"Xavier?" Candy said, folding her arms across her chest. "I had a gay husband before. I'd know."

"These people will do whatever they can to get ahead."

Candy stared at Darcy, whose face turned redder with each word.

"Xavier may be a ladies' man, but he is also one of the richest directors in this town," said Darcy. "If he wants to keep working, he's going to have to give it up at some point. That's how it is out here. Unless you are some angel sent from God himself, he's never going to change. He'll do what he has to do. Including taking you along the ride with him. Watch yourself."

Candy thought about Darcy's words after she left. She recalled the gala, but nothing stood out to her. Nothing in the last several months, except that he did glance at Elena's chest that night, but so did several men. Xavier seemed more determined, every day, and drinking an unusual amount of alcohol, but she chalked it up to work. Could it be more? Anything was possible.

"Monsieur Rogers is waiting for you in the next room." This announcement came from the butler to Cleveland's grand suite at the St. Regis.

She had stared at Cleveland's invitation for the last few days, hand delivered to her during a day when Xavier was out of town. And now she had decided to respond. She wasn't twenty-five years old anymore and felt confident she wouldn't be taken in by his charms anymore. She thought about all the possible scenarios that could happen. What did he have to say that required an in-person visit?

He headed toward her and wrapped her up in his arms. Her body tightened.

"You look delicious," he whispered.

"Cleveland. Please. You are still married. I'm married. We can't be doing this."

"You can't make me believe you've completely forgotten me," he said.

Candy melted in his arms, relaxing with every breath. They hadn't been alone like this in years. She had never forgotten him, but she didn't answer.

"Now, look at you," he said, looking her over. "The most desirable wife on the West Coast."

"Don't you forget it," Candy said.

His fingers lightly touched her wavy brown tresses. She remembered how she used to lay her head on his shoulder after she had returned from another awful trip at her mom's house. He used to rub her head and listen to her sobs, and he never once judged. She pulled her head back and separated herself from him.

"No," Candy said, pulling her shoulders back. "I can't do this. I can't let this happen. I'm married to Xavier."

His face changed. "I understand." He smirked. "How much time do you have?"

"Enough."

He rubbed her shoulders, and she stiffened again.

"What happened to Marlene?" Candy said in a low voice as they walked to the sofa.

He poured two glasses of whiskey. "I had a good talk with her. You'll never hear from her again. Let's put it that way," he said, circling the glass with his hand.

Candy nodded. "So, I'm good, then? She won't go blabbing our business, or my business and what I do."

"No," Cleveland said, piercing her with his eyes. "And let's talk about your latest business."

"Xavier?" Candy added.

"Why him?" Cleveland frowned.

"Why not?"

"He's a hot head. He was a Hollywood playboy, and he's got a temper. Still, I've got to say, you can't get any higher than him, profile-wise. You may start getting invitations from Saudi princes next."

Candy inhaled deeply. "I think this may be my last. I'm just getting tired."

"You're falling in love?"

"I've gotten everything a woman can dream about. Several homes, millions in the bank, stocks, bonds, retirement three times over. And I've been to the most lavish parties, islands, and homes. I've met the most amazing people."

"And?" he looked at her, hanging on.

"And I still want more. I want a normal marriage. Real love."

"With Xavier?"

"No," she said quickly.

They both knew neither of them were spring chickens anymore. Being with one person was more attractive now than ever.

Cleveland took a sip from his glass. "Don't fall in love. With him."

"Did you follow your own advice?" she asked him, referring to how he felt about her.

He huffed and reached back for his glass. "I love you, Candy. More now than ever before. Can you love for real?"

"I have, and I do," she said, staring him down.

They both fell silent, suspended in their own thoughts.

Then Cleveland said, "Keep an eye on Xavier. I'll be here for you when you are ready."

"Ready?"

Cleveland seemed to catch himself. "As a friend, of course."

Candy cut her eyes away. "Yes, right."

Then he asked, "Do you have Xavier in therapy? If he's becoming too much, you can get him under control."

"No," Candy said. "He's home most of the time, and when he's not he checks in. He's been doing good, and I'd like to think it is because of me."

"You can't make anyone better than they want to be."

"I got Xavier handled."

"*Stay* in control. And keep friends out of it."

Candy sipped her drink, understanding who he meant.

"But," Cleveland said, crossing his tall, strapping legs, "I did notice that since you came into the picture, all his press has been clean. That big contract renewal he scored with Ben on board, he's been dealing with big things. He wouldn't have done it without you." Cleveland smiled warmly at her. "And you, with him, as a Black couple is powerful in this town."

"And that's why I respect Xavier. He's wants to be with a Black woman. He believes in it. Staying true is very important to him."

"Uhm, I wouldn't go too far," Cleveland said with a grin.

"Xavier is a man who needs a wife," Candy observed. "What can I say? Without one, he has no focus. I trained him with the press, introduced him to a few people, and I'm making the most of *my* time."

"Like hell you are," Cleveland interrupted. "You're living in one of the richest zip codes in the country, you get every need catered, and you get to say when it ends." He raised his glass to meet hers. "I've been around a little longer than you, and men like Xavier return to their tomcat ways. And when he does, I will be here for you. All of me."

Candy felt her presence expand like light filling her up from the inside. *All of him.* That was all she ever wanted.

25

It was after dinner when Candy arrived back home. Xavier's car was parked in the driveway. She grabbed her cell phone and noticed several missed calls from him and Elena.

She climbed out of the car, and the brisk night hair tussled her tresses. She promised herself she'd call Elena as soon as she got inside. She took a deep breath as she marched up the steps, silently beating herself up for missing the calls. She prayed everything was all right.

As she walked in, she heard tears, then Xavier's voice talking to a woman that sounded like Elena across the hall in the kitchen. As much as she wanted to join them, she stood back and listened with her head slightly arched toward the kitchen.

"Man, what an asshole," Xavier said, comforting Elena. Candy could see from the reflection in the foyer mirror that she had her head on his shoulders, and he had a hand on her shoulder.

"He did this to me before. I hate him," Elena cried, holding a wad of tissue to her nose.

Whatever happened must have been devastating, Candy thought as her stomach churned. As much as she felt badly, though, her insides were fuming at Elena dragging Xavier into this. Or was this her way of getting back to her after Michael?

"Thank you again for picking me up. I called Candy, but—"

Candy slowly walked to the kitchen. "Did someone mention my name?" She placed her handbag on the island.

Elena immediately moved away from Xavier, a hint of guilt on her face. "I called you." Elena scowled at Candy. "Michael kicked me out. I had no place to go."

Xavier and Candy locked eyes over Elena. He slipped off the island chair and surrendered it to Candy. "I'm gonna leave you two alone. Candy, if she wants to stay here for the night, it's okay with me. Good night, ladies."

"Hungry?" Candy asked, annoyance in her voice at Elena's reaction to her. "We have steak from last night's dinner."

"No, I'm fine." Elena wiped her tears. "Sorry, I couldn't wait for you to call me. I called Xavier."

"You heard Xavier. You can stay for the night."

"Candy, I know you're mad. Don't act like you're not."

Candy tightened her mouth as she breathed through her nose.

"Well, let it out. My night can't get any worse."

"What do you plan to do? You can't blow up your life and spill it out all over mine."

Elena nodded, wiping her nose. "I had no one else to call."

"Just like Michael had no one else to call?"

Elena stayed quiet.

"For tonight only, Elena."

Candy grabbed her bag. "Look, here," she said, writing a check to Elena. "Find a place. You need to be safe."

Elena took the check, and her eyes welled up again. "Thank you, Candy." She reached to hug her, but Candy stepped back.

"Greta can show you the guest room and get you set up. You work in the morning?"

Elena folded the check in half and put it away. "I do."

"She can do a wakeup call for you and prepare breakfast if you like. Do you need anything else?" Candy said in a weary voice.

"No," Elena said, forcing a smile. "You've been kind enough."

Candy pressed the intercom and instructed Greta to help Elena settle in.

"Then good night. And," Candy said, turning back around, "sorry about you and Michael. He said things were different with you, too. I just didn't realize how bad."

Candy walked up the steps. She couldn't get to bed any faster.

"How's she?" Xavier asked when she walked into the bedroom. He was already settled in bed with his work notepad.

"You look mighty comfy," Candy said in a snide tone, kicking off her shoes.

"What was I supposed to do, leave her in the streets?" he asked. "Besides, where were you?"

"I was meeting an old friend." Candy was not going to allow him to change the subject. She turned on the shower. "Look, it's fine. Thank you for letting her stay."

"No problem, but after tomorrow, she's got to go."

Candy slipped off her panties and bra, and let them fall to the ground. "I'm pissed she did this. She'll be okay, though."

Candy stepped in the shower, lights off, and let the water run all over her body, cleansing every part of her that weighed her down. An image of Xavier comforting Elena ran through her mind. She thought about something else to distract her.

In a few minutes, Xavier joined her, gently massaging between her thighs until she relaxed in his arms, sinking her body deeper into his. She released everything to him, bringing chills down her spine. After, he laid her on the bed and their bodies joined in heated rhythm with each other.

26

Candy drove by her house in Malibu. It was a little more than an hour away from Xavier's, and she hadn't been back since they married. She also hadn't rented it out as much as she thought she would. She parked in front and admired the sound of the surf hitting the shore and the colorful flowers decorating the landscape. A feeling of tranquility overcame her. She dug in her bag for the keys.

She turned the lock and walked inside. A clean, minty scent floated in the air. Adrianna was the housemaid, and from the smell, she had just left. Candy had hired a small staff to watch the home and keep it tidy, but she crept around as if she was the stranger. She walked lightly, peering and peeking in the rooms. Everything looked the same, she told herself.

She sunk onto one of her lush, thick sofas and disappeared among the pillows and throws. "Mmm," she said, feeling free, hopeful. She brought a purple throw to her nose and inhaled it. It was her favorite, with gold trimmings and an Indian Aztec pattern. Greg had bought it for her on one of his trips, monogrammed.

Candy gazed up at the stained-glass skylight window. She didn't care that the rush-hour traffic would take her twice as long to make it back home.

As she lay there, however, a new feeling came over her, one of intense loneliness.

Until her phone rang.

"Candy, so sorry to call this early," Lettie said, sounding out of breath.

"Are you okay?" Candy asked.

"It's the workmen you hired to lay the new roof. They are here for their money, and Mommy hasn't paid them!"

"What did she do with all that money?"

"I don't know. She had to give them something to start the job, but—"

"How much does she owe them?"

"Twenty-five thousand dollars?"

"How is that possible?" Candy ran all the numbers in her head. She calculated exactly what they needed. "I didn't see twenty-five thousand dollars' worth of damages."

"Well, it is. There's mold. Looks like it's been there forever. They said they have to do it or else report the house unsafe."

"Is that her in the background?"

"Yes, she is cussing them out. They are threatening to call the police because she owes them money."

"I'll be right there."

Candy grabbed her bag and bolted out the door as fast as she could. She was farther away than she liked, but in a half hour she was there. She hoped the worst had passed.

When she arrived, cop cars were outside the house. All her hopes were dashed.

A tall, burly officer with a white and pepper beard walked toward her, with Lettie by his side.

"Officer, what is happening?" Candy asked, scanning the cop cars.

"Are you the daughter responsible for this?"

She wiped her hair away from her face and pulled out her purse. "I'm here to pay who needs to be paid, if that's what you mean."

"These gentlemen need to be paid. And your mom assaulted one of them, as well."

"Oh no, officer, that must be a mistake."

"It's not," said an older gentleman, dressed in a white and red plaid shirt and jeans, approaching them. "But I'm not pressing any charges. Don't you worry, Ms. Robertson. But we did have to call the cops to get a handle on this."

"Mr. Burns. Here's the rest of the money."

"Ms. Robertson, thank you."

"Where's Mommy?" Candy turned to Lettie.

"Inside."

Lettie led her inside where her mother sat on the couch in her pink house robe, white hair bonnet and slippers, as if she didn't have a care in the world.

"Mommy, what the hell?" Candy said, marching toward her mother. "What did you do with the money from last time?"

"I paid the bills. They quoted me one thing and now another."

"That is not true. Mr. Burns is a good man."

Candy's mom sneered. "What's the big deal. You paid them, right?"

"I did because I want you and Lettie to stay in this house safely. But this is it. I'm done."

"You prefer your rich Hollywood friends anyway."

"That's all you can say. Do you know you could have been arrested today?"

Her mother breathed out loudly, and said, "It wouldn't be the first time."

"What are you doing, putting your hands on people?"

Her mother put out her cigarette. "I have no problem fighting my own battles." She started to walk upstairs.

"Mommy, you don't have to leave. We can all talk this through," said Lettie.

"I've had enough of you two. My hands may slip and slap somebody."

Lettie and Candy were left downstairs. Candy looked out the

window. The workmen descended on the house to continue their work. "You want to get out of here for a bit?" Candy asked Lettie. "You can drive back with me."

"Nah, I'm heading back to campus."

"Good. We'll talk later."

She and Candy left in their separate directions. They both had had enough, neither believing their mother would ever see beyond what's in front of her.

27

————————

While looking through her new apartment window and sipping her morning coffee, Elena ran through the day in her head. She dutifully got an apartment fifteen minutes away from Xavier's studio. The location made it a cinch to come for lunch and go back home to Michael and the kids in just a half hour. What she liked most was the proximity to the studio. She worked late as needed and didn't have to worry about driving at night, which she hated. It was farther away from Candy than she would have liked, but maybe, she thought, she needed that, too.

Finding her own way never came easy, and if she had to start now, so be it.

She dabbed a fresh coat of red on her lips, grabbed her keys, makeup bag, and purse. In a few minutes, she pulled into the parking lot, one of only a few cars, including Xavier's. As she parked and made her way to the craft services area for breakfast, she spotted Xavier sipping a cup of coffee as he walked back to his trailer.

"Xavier!" she called out, waving.

He turned around and motioned for her to join him. They both walked across the sunny lot, talking about their day ahead.

"How's the new apartment coming?" he asked.

"Like a dream. It's so easy to get here. I have quiet neighbors and, most important, peace of mind," she said, sliding her hands in the back pockets of her dark, skinny jeans.

"Peace of mind is priceless. Congrats again," he said, stopping at the door of his trailer.

"Would you like to see it some time?" she asked, nervous about being too forward.

He chuckled, looking at her. "You know, Elena. You're one interesting lady. You want to come inside and join me for another cup of coffee?"

Elena looked around.

"Don't worry. It's okay. Our schedule was pushed back today. We have time."

Elena marched up the steps behind him as he closed the door. Paul was in the back, working on a laptop, and didn't even look up at them.

Xavier showed her the rundown for the day. Elena pretended to listen, but she couldn't focus. His Dior smell from his freshly shaven skin, up against his sky-blue collared shirt, made her surprisingly giddy. She couldn't stand still.

"You okay?"

"Yeah," she replied, "just a bit hot in here. What is the AC on, a hundred?"

"There's no AC in here."

"Oh," she said as they both looked at each other. She lowered her eyes from his face. Lucky Candy. He was absolutely delicious.

"Anyway, like I was saying—"

Elena didn't know what came over as she asked, "Do you want to have lunch today? I made baklava, and I have some leftovers. Taking the rest to the kids tonight. Think of it as a thank you for picking me up when things got bad."

Xavier gave her a half-smile. "Sure."

～

Around midday, Elena joined Xavier for lunch in his trailer. She unwrapped the fresh-smelling baklava and took out a piece.

"Out of all the exotic foods I tried, I don't think I've had baklava. I'm curious," he said, taking it from her.

"Oh, you will love it. Especially my baklava. Just the right amount of sweetness," she smiled, urging him.

He took a generous bite, and a few flakes stuck to his lips. "Mmm, this is delicious. Tastes so fresh. And you made these?"

"I love to bake. When I have the time." She pulled two napkins from her bag and dabbed the flakes from his mouth.

He took her wrist. "You don't have to do that. I got it."

"It's gone now." She smiled nervously. "I'm a mom. I can't help myself sometimes."

Xavier bit into the baklava again. "Man, you need to share this with the crew. They appreciate a good dessert."

"Anytime," she said, packing away her lunch. Xavier did the same. Though his was simpler. A turkey sandwich on rye that he already finished.

Elena looked at her watch. They still had about another forty minutes together. As Xavier drank his coffee and baklava, she could feel a sense of ease between them. She felt drawn to him. More every day.

"Xavier, I really like spending time with you," she said. She moved in closer to him, and he did the same.

"I do, too," he said. "There's something easy about you. I feel relaxed. Candy is lucky to have you."

"But she's not the only one who can have me." As soon as Elena said that, she felt awful. And she looked away, embarrassed.

He laughed. "Don't worry. I know what you mean. But do you think that's a good idea?"

Betraying Candy had never crossed her mind. Candy had been her friend for ages. But they were grown women, and the stakes were high. It was be happy now or die trying. And she wasn't going to die trying. Not anymore. At almost forty, she had to take life by the neck, and as a young Romanian girl growing up in the village, she took horses down by their necks. She didn't have room for fear. Candy would find another man, another client easily, she thought. This marriage wasn't real. Right?

Elena drew her body closer to Xavier, who let her get as close as she wanted. She put her nose to his, then lips, lightly touching his to sense how far he'd go. She parted her lips, and he did his. She took her hand and cupped his head, massaging it, and she inhaled him.

Then he pushed back some. "Elena," he said, breathing hard. They looked at each other. "I gotta go. I'm planning a party for Candy, and I—"

"I'm sorry," she said. "Forget this happened."

Xavier quickly left the trailer.

28

Candy had caught a whiff of Xavier planning her fortieth birthday bash a few days before, but she preferred a nice dinner in town.

Xavier stepped out of the shower after his morning run and pulled something out of the closet. "Happy birthday, Beautiful," he said, handing her a bouquet of red roses and an envelope.

Candy wiped her sleepy eyes, refusing to believe that her fortieth had quietly arrived. She opened one eye as Xavier covered her in kisses.

"Thank you," she said, feeling like she had landed in a rose garden surrounded by a delicious, fragrant bouquet. There must have been almost a hundred roses in the bundle.

She read the small note card.

Your presence is requested at your fortieth Birthday Bash. Dress is formal, but you can be as sexy as you want. Where? Home. Love, Xavier.

Candy turned to Xavier. His long, muscular brown legs peeked out from under the towel. She gave him a kiss of approval on the lips, but she felt something off. She opted to see, but not see. She was not ruining today.

His thick, warm lips covered hers. Of all his many assets, Xavier was an expert kisser, leading with gentleness and a precision that seemed to want to open up every secret she'd ever had. Soon, Candy felt herself softening into his thoughtful gesture.

A knock on the door surprised them. Xavier slipped on his boxers.

Greta walked in with a breakfast of waffles, champagne, and fruit. "Happy birthday, Mrs. Oshun." Greta laughed. "I give you your favorite breakfast."

With profuse thanks, Candy opened her arms to receive the decadent display.

After setting down the tray on the bed, Greta left them alone.

Candy slipped the covers off and dived into her breakfast with some help from Xavier. He cut up her waffles and fed her strawberries. Then he kissed the sweet, strawberry juices from the corner of her mouth.

"Xavier, come on now," Candy said, keeping him at arm's length. "You threw a birthday party on me a few minutes ago. A girl needs to know what to wear. How long do I have?"

"I have everything picked out for you. You don't have to do anything," Xavier said, enjoying Candy's curiosity.

"I can pick out my own clothes," she reminded him, forking up a generous serving of waffles.

"But it's your birthday. I don't want you to worry about anything. If you don't like it, you don't have to wear it. I also have a hair and nail stylist coming in a few hours."

What Xavier had in mind was starting to sound good. Almost as good as breakfast.

Xavier sent a text, and within seconds, someone knocked at the door. It opened again.

"Madam?" said a handsome man wearing a black beret. He was tall and slim and held a Jean Paul Gaultier box and a Christian Louboutin box.

"Oh my God," Candy said, dropping her fork. "What is this?"

The man left two boxes at her bedside and left.

"Open them," Xavier said, his handsome smile showing his row of perfect white teeth.

Candy flipped open the Gaultier box to find the most exquisite red and gold cocktail dress, shimmery and lavished with bits of leather.

"Xavier!" she shouted. "I would never have bought this for myself."

She gently pulled the dressy number out of the box, crawled out of bed, and held it up against her. "And I love it!" She twirled around with it like she was nine years old all over again.

Xavier brought the Louboutin box to her and watched as Candy lost herself in her excitement. Inside the box was the latest pair of shimmery Louboutin open-toed high heels to match the dress. She slipped her slender foot into the shoes. They fit perfectly. Then she slid into the dress.

Candy looked in the mirror. "I'd never wear red and leather together, or these heels. So why do I love these so much?" She looked at him. "Thank you," she said, putting her arms around him.

It was times like these that she relished, the good surprises, where a marriage would push her to discover something she'd never know otherwise, even if it was only a dress. It helped her get to know another side of herself that she had never met.

"Be ready at eight," Xavier said just before he landed a long, lingering kiss on her lips.

"And who's coming?"

Xavier rubbed his sharp, chiseled chin. "You'll see."

"Did you call my sister?"

"Oh, I forgot."

"Humpf," Candy said. "I'll text her. But no more surprises." She sent Lettie a quick text inviting her over and offering a car to pick her up.

BY EIGHT, she looked out the window at the Rolls-Royces and Range Rovers easing up to the front door for the valet. She heard banter from upstairs, the happy laughter and high-pitched voices that seemed to be calling out her name. But they weren't.

Her nails and hair had never looked better. She gazed into the mirror and ran her hand over her smoothed edges, one part of her hair swooped to the side. Her nails were neatly manicured, dazzled with a cranberry red that complemented her dress to the hilt.

Her skin felt like silk, scrubbed to almost deadening relaxation for over an hour. A Korean spa specialist, one of the most sought after in Hollywood, had bathed her. Her face was steamed to a smooth, glowing complexion that made it look as if she had spent a week cruising the waters of Monaco. Her makeup highlighted all her beauty, from the curve of her eyebrow to her pouty lips, coated in a luscious, rubies-infused lipstick. It was vitamin-rich, gold-encased, and organic, and cost over two thousand dollars a stick. The makeup artist gifted it to her.

If anyone had once doubted that Candy was well taken care of, they didn't anymore. She had become exactly what she had imagined as that lost nine-year-old. She built her life for these moments, when she looked into the mirror and saw the fruits of her labor instead of what she had sacrificed.

She heard a knock on the door and spun around in her vanity chair.

Her escort, a short but handsome man in a tuxedo, held his arm out to walk her. "They are waiting for you, Mrs. Oshun."

Candy slipped her arm into his. As they walked to the top of the staircase, she saw the array of guests of all colors, backgrounds, and stature. The staircase banister was trimmed with shimmery white crystals. She took each step deliberately, regally, holding on tightly to her escort and taking everything in all at once. The home had been transformed into a scene from *Coming to America*, with flecks of gold and diamonds everywhere. A trio of dancers with conga players at the bottom of the steps serenaded her in an African dance as she walked down.

Huge paintings of Candy were positioned on platforms for people to study and admire. Where did he get these? she wondered. As Candy reached the bottom of the stairs, a young girl dressed in white appeared holding a black box.

Candy didn't know if her feet were touching the floor. The winding staircase and the opulence of the evening made her feel a bit dizzy. She thought it was a bit too much. She was turning forty, not being crowned queen of England.

"Happy Birthday!" everyone shouted.

She scanned the crowd for anyone she knew, but there was really no one. The crowd applauded again, smiling warmly at her. Lettie hadn't confirmed she was coming, but sent her happy birthday wishes earlier.

"Happy Birthday," said the young girl with the box. Candy had never seen this girl in her life.

Who are you? she thought. If she stayed with Xavier, this would be her life, full, with new people to meet and get to know. Maybe she could even have another friend.

"Speech, speech!"

Xavier stood beside her. Candy opened the box to find a dazzling white diamond necklace with a big white diamond pendant. She nearly lost her breath. "This is spell-binding," she said, turning to Xavier.

They kissed. Then he draped the necklace round her neck. There were a few appreciative nods, and, of course, the envious eyes of women with forced smiles that would give anything to find out how Candy had landed such a man.

"Thank you, I lo—" she said under her breath, overcome with love for him before nearly kicking herself. An armed man, about six-foot-six, came over and slipped off the necklace. She handed the box to him.

"Weird," she said to Xavier. "Really?"

"Don't worry, you can keep it. We just have to guard it tonight."

"Right." She gritted her teeth.

"You were about to say something before he came?" He peered into her eyes.

The moment had passed. "Oh, nothing. We should mingle, yes?"

"Come, let me introduce you."

Xavier took her around the room to meet the most important people in attendance. Mostly business, as usual.

She eyed several sumptuous bouquets at the door, a few of which Greta was still arranging in vases.

She knew no one. "Did you invite Elena at least?" she asked.

"Of course, there she is," Xavier said, pointing at the door.

An hour late, Elena had finally arrived. Candy darted in her direction.

They embraced as soon as they were in reach of each other.

"I knew you were too quiet today!" Candy said, relieved to have her friend with her, someone she knew. She grabbed Elena's hand.

"So sorry I'm late. I couldn't decide what to wear," Elena said, out of breath.

"Everything okay?" She noticed an elegance in Elena she hadn't seen in a while. She looked statuesque and cool in a strapless black dress. "You're glowing all over in that dress."

"Thank you, but yours is even better," Elena said, taking a glass of champagne from one of the waiters who walked around the room. "Is this a coronation party or what?"

"That's what I thought." Candy shook her head. "It's too much, and I've had everything."

"Girl, stop complaining," Elena said as they drifted to a corner and sat down. Here, Candy was finally free from all the industry banter. Elena took a long sip from her champagne and grabbed a filet mignon delicacy from another passing tray. "I would give up all I have to spend a day in your shoes."

Candy threw her head back a few inches. "Elena, you have several times," she laughed. "Literally."

"True, true," Elena said, as they laughed.

"Me, too," Candy said, adjusting her dress.

Xavier walked up to them. "You ladies enjoying the evening? Especially our birthday girl here."

Before Candy could answer, Elena answered, "Yes." She embraced Xavier until they both sat down.

Candy scooted over. She noticed something new in both of their faces, but she couldn't put a finger on it. But the closeness wasn't too strange. They did work together after all, she reasoned.

Candy chatted with another guest while keeping her eye on Xavier and Elena the whole time. What Cleveland had said rang in her ears. *Men like Xavier always return to their tomcat ways.*

29

On a sweltering hot Labor Day weekend, days after her birthday party, Candy found herself alone in bed. Xavier had left town for a meeting the day after her birthday bash.

Candy closed the blinds to keep out some of the morning sun then sent a text to hold breakfast off for a few hours. She called her sister.

"How are you?" she asked when Lettie picked up.

Lettie sighed, "I really wanted to make your birthday party. Too tired."

"I'll survive. But, how are you? We haven't really talked with everything going on with the house."

"The roof is almost done."

"Back to you?" Candy asked with a smile in her voice.

"I figured I'll share one disaster at a time."

"Is it the guy you're seeing?"

"No, he's been great. But I am late on tuition."

"How?"

"Mommy found the money you been depositing."

"Is she a holder on the account? I thought you took her off."

"I did, too, but I guess I forgot to send back in the signed papers."

Candy fixed her lips to get upset but realized it wasn't worth it.

"Where is Lettie's money?" Candy demanded as she busted through her mother's bedroom door. "As a matter of fact, where is my money?"

"You can't come up in here like this," her mother said, pulling her robe together. "I told Lettie I would pay her back."

"You mean pay me back."

"Please. It's not like you need it."

With her hands on her hips, Candy let her have it. "What is really going on with you? I can't keep taking care of you. I have my own life!"

"You call what you have a life? All of these men who buy you. You are a disgrace to me and this family!"

"Then why have anything to do with me? Why take my money if you hate me so much?"

"You give marriage or any possibility of love a bad name. God knows what you have put in Lettie's mind. She's bound to turn out like you."

"Better me than you."

Her mother whipped her neck around. "You think you are a bag of chips and Kool-Aid, don't you? Well, let me tell you. That African prince you sold yourself to is gonna end up using you and going back to his old ways. He'll end up with somebody he really loves."

That burned Candy. It echoed what Cleveland warned her about.

"At least I am true to myself. I may be a bitch. I may be lousy with money. But I know my worth," her mother added.

"Oh really? At least the men in my life are worth something. We make each other better. What did you get?"

Her mother looked at her up and down. "Exactly."

Candy couldn't take it anymore. She was on the verge of truly hurting her mom but not as much as her mother had just hurt her.

Candy marched back down the stairs "We're going to the bank, Lettie. That money is definitely gone."

CANDY AND LETTIE met with a teller who broke down where the deposits went. Straight to her mom's account. She promptly set up another account for Lettie and deposited the check into that.

Lettie's tears welled up in her eyes. "I hate that every time we are together, it's over something bad. I really do."

"This is temporary. Once you graduate, you'll be on your own. You'll have a good job. I can help out if you need it. But you got to start preparing yourself to be out there without me one day."

As for her mother, Candy didn't know when she'd ever see her again.

30

Elena had waited weeks to thank Candy formally for arranging the job with Xavier. They hadn't been able to pin down a date until now.

She always made a point of arriving at places before Candy. She enjoyed watching her walk in a room and the way the men and even women looked at her. She had an aura that surrounded her that Elena couldn't explain, but she hoped to imbibe a little bit of it each time they spent together.

Candy walked in, on time, in a casual white and blue jumpsuit that accented her waist, thick sunglasses, and a low-key designer wristlet bag. Her hair was gathered on her shoulders. Elena wore a black maxi dress with a simple red lipstick and a pair of Jimmy Choos that Candy gave her years ago.

The waiter guided Candy to the seat and placed two menus down in front of them. They hugged as they settled in.

"What is my budget?" Candy said, studying the menu, one she was familiar with, as they've been to this place before.

"No budget this time," Elena said.

"That's easy, then. I'll take the sautéed scallops, polenta, and greens. A glass of prosecco," Candy read off.

"I'll take the same," Elena said as she pushed her menu to the side. She noticed a tension in Candy's voice as she gave her order.

Candy took a swig of water, then looked up. "I guess things are looking up for you. New apartment. New you."

Elena winced. "Yes, I guess you can say that. I do feel like a new me. I really need to be on my own."

Candy asked. "Without the kids?"

"Well, for now. I am thinking about a lot. What I want and don't want. How have *you* been?"

"My mom and I had this terrible fight, and I don't know if I'll ever be able to forgive her."

Elena grabbed her own water glass and took a long sip before she began. "I would have come with you. You should have asked. I know it can be hard with your mom."

Candy stared at her long and hard. "Elena, I don't know what's been going on lately with us. I just feel like we're different now. Both of us. Like you are not being totally honest with me."

Elena scrambled, wondering if she should admit it or not. Her interactions with Xavier. "I have a lot on my mind. I still can't get over how Michael reached out to you about me. And you didn't tell me."

Candy squinted in confusion. "So that is still an issue?"

Elena felt it was a stretch, but she wanted to show Candy everything wasn't perfect between them. She just wasn't sure if she could prove it. "I still think about it."

Candy laughed lightly. "Great."

"Look, I wanted this lunch to be a thank you. I don't want us to get off on a bad foot. I've been working a lot on the set. And I want this to really work, Candy. I need this job."

Candy took a deep breath. "Sure, you're welcome. I just hope I won't regret it. I don't want you to sacrifice your family."

Elena cracked a smile. "Michael and I had problems before this job. And I really want to thank you so much. I don't ever want you to feel I take our friendship for granted."

Candy nodded. She then decided to offer something that had been on her mind, too. "Xavier has been talking about you. He said you swooped in to do Alfre Woodard at the last minute when her makeup artist was a no-show."

"I was so nervous. Her skin is gorgeous. She thanked me a million times," Elena said, recalling how proud it made her feel.

"You really saved the day on that one. Xavier said she wants to work with you *only* from now on."

"I can't believe it, either. It's crazy what's happening. These are things I only dreamed about."

"You deserve it, Elena. You really do," Candy said, finally smiling. "But keep away from Xavier. It doesn't look good."

"What do you mean?"

"He's saying that you are around him a lot. He feels uncomfortable," Candy lied. She wanted to see Elena's reaction.

"It's true. I am kind of enamored of him. I'm learning so much. I did have lunch with him the other day. I hope that is okay. No?"

"Xavier can be very charming. Don't confuse his charm for interest."

"I'm not interested in him like that. Yes, he is charming, but you know I would never mess with any of your clients."

Candy stared at her. "And that's why I trust you."

"None of this would have happened without you. I still had some of my old makeup tricks, but I have learned so much on Xavier's set. He only works with the best, and I see why. I am so grateful to have you," she paused, "and Xavier in my life."

The waiter approached at that exact time and took their orders.

"What is up with Cleveland?"

"Cleveland is Cleveland. He and Marlene probably won't last the rest of the year. I just know it," Candy said, but she kept any other thoughts to herself. She noticed Elena's keen interest in him lately, too, and what she felt about him.

"I'm still thinking about that Bright Hope gala, I feel different ever since that night. Like anything is possible. I have some money now, I have my own place. No kids. And I have to figure out my life if Michael and I divorce."

Candy inhaled her glass of prosecco in one swallow. "Don't throw your family away over what you saw. It is not free. It comes with a price."

"So be it. I can start over. I can be better for me and for my kids in the future."

In a low, steady voice, Candy said, "Your kids are young enough to know and old enough to never forgive you for this."

31

———————

Elena lay in bed that night in a state of excitement. Her mind sped with visions of what would come next. She couldn't hide it anymore. She spent more time with Xavier every day, working on the set, having lunch when they could. Her longing was more than she could ever imagine, and she wondered what Xavier felt. She did know that he never turned down her invitations.

Her phone rang.

"You forgot your makeup kit on the set tonight. I know how you are about bringing it home."

"Oh," Elena said, jumping out of bed. "My mind must have been elsewhere. I know it's pretty late. But I can come right over and get it. I have thousands of dollars' worth of makeup in there."

"Don't worry. I'll stop by and drop it off on my way home."

Elena hopped out of bed and began to look for clothes to wear. But something stopped her. She looked at herself in the mirror and decided to keep her purple silk nightgown on. Instead, she tucked away some dirty dishes in the dishwasher, and gargled with Listerine. She passed a brush over her long, thick black locks. She wanted to look effortless, like him coming by didn't change anything. She grabbed her black silk robe, put it on but leaving it open.

In less than twenty minutes, Xavier was at her door.

"Here you go," he said, handing her the bag as he stood on her doorstep. "It was open when I found it."

Elena took the bag, briefly examined it, and exhaled in relief. "It looks like everything is in there," she said, the front of her robe opening slightly from the breeze outside.

"Okay, well, I guess I'll head out. Candy doesn't like it when I get home after midnight."

Elena opened her apartment door a little farther. "Why don't you come in, for like five minutes?"

"I can't Elena, I gotta head back—"

Elena reached for his hand, pulling him into her apartment, and closed the door.

Xavier sat down on the couch. He watched Elena's hips as she went into the kitchen and fixed them two glasses of wine. Being a faithful husband was new to him, and tonight, he thought he might fail miserably.

"This is a nice, cozy spot," he said, looking around. "Feels like the perfect bachelor pad."

"I know it's small, but it's enough for now," she said, handing him the sweet wine. "Do you want me to call Candy and tell her you're here?"

"No." He shook his head. "I'm not staying."

Elena took his hand, and he coolly took her in as she rose to meet him. She inhaled his Dior scent, and her eyes scanned his broad shoulders. She slipped her robe off, exposing the top of her breasts. "Can you stay a little while longer? I don't like sleeping alone." She looked at him with pleading eyes. Her body tingled with his essence hovering around her.

He inhaled deeply, looking at her breasts that seemed to rise with each breath she took.

Elena wrapped her arms around him. It was bold, but shyness didn't get her this far, she thought. "Be with me."

"Elena, I—"

She brought her fingers to his lips. With the other hand, she dimmed the lights.

"Just between us." She took his finger and sucked on it.

She pulled Xavier gently to the bedroom by his collar as she walked backward, keeping her eyes on him. "I've wanted you since day one."

Xavier didn't say a word but closed his eyes as Elena laid him on the bed. She slipped off her robe and nightie, revealing everything. She climbed on top of him, undoing his shirt one button at a time.

32

Xavier felt a lump in his throat his entire car ride home the next morning for work. He had come home late and slipped into the shower, then bed, without Candy saying a word. But he knew he had a major fail on his conscience, and even worse, with someone who worked for him. His mind raced with Elena's image. She was gorgeous, and he wanted her, but he couldn't feel the same detachment he could muster up in situations like this in the past. This was Candy. He wished he had never gone by Elena's apartment.

When Xavier first met Candy, he thought he had found everything he wanted. She was gorgeous, smart, exuberant. She was an insider's woman only known by the right people. And if you didn't know Candy, then you weren't on the inside. Xavier had been fighting to be on the inside in Hollywood for over a decade since his Nigerian film days. He had tried dating, but the women seemed shallow and dense. His parents tried, but the women were too traditional, boring. He tried picking up women at parties, but that only lasted for the night. He noticed that all the really successful people were partnered either by arrangement or sheer will. His volcanic temper helped make the perfect excuse for his single status. He gave the perception of being unattainable, too hot to handle.

But that could only last so long. In this town, Xavier knew he had to stay new to stay relevant. When he heard that Candy was available for marriage again, he slipped in. His publicist tracked her down and got him what he needed. He thought long and hard about it. What he wanted. It was important to him to have a Black wife. As a child, he had dreamed of being part of a Black power couple. Once he was on a date with a bombshell redhead when a beautiful Black woman with shapely legs, thick, luscious hair, and a vibrant laugh walked by with a friend. He nearly broke his neck looking her way. He loved Black women, everything about them, from how easily they could drop into rhythm to almost any beat to how their velvety brown skin draped their curves. The darker the woman, the better for Xavier. If he wasn't Black himself, he would definitely have a fetish.

Candy nearly checked every box, except she wasn't really his—a hundred percent. Her reputation preceded her, and he was intimidated by what she knew about him—or what she knew, period. Her sophistication and ease with people were what he needed most. He wished he could be that way with people, easy. Except his anxiety never quit.

Secretly, he hoped Candy would fall in love and drop the contract. That they could forget the arrangement and stay together. He needed Candy to save him from himself. He needed Candy to help him grow. And that she did. He promised himself that he would take care of her, be one of her best husbands, maybe even for life.

Then Elena came along. His first thought was to say no when Candy asked about the job, but he thought doing so would make Candy more invested in their relationship—except Elena became invested in *him*. He admired her work ethic, her simple style and her motherly ways. It surprised him.

At work, and on the set, people waved at him, some nodded. Others wished him a good evening. That kind of stuff never happened before Candy, he thought. His world felt kinder. People were attracted him, good people. Except for the occasional tantrums, and he had curbed those to only once every few months instead of once a day.

As he hopped into his truck, he thought about ways he could get Candy to stay. He had to stop his affair with Elena. But he felt drawn in by her, intoxicated.

In a few months, he would have to go back out on the market. His reputation would be repaired, and he would do anything to keep it like that. But he wasn't eager to start dating again. He knew women were just waiting.

XAVIER PULLED up to his publicist's office. Ginnie and he were scheduled to meet to discuss the upcoming end of his marriage.

"Hey, my African prince," Ginnie said as she reached up to hug him. Ginnie was an old school, sixty-ish Jewish publicist who had been in the industry for decades, having repped the biggest actors in the business. "You look more handsome every day."

"How's Charles?" Xavier asked, referring to her husband of over forty years.

"If he could eat eggplant parmesan every day for breakfast, he would be fine. I swear that man has the palette of a goldfish."

Xavier smiled. "That must be nice." They chatted about their families some more, until Ginnie got to the point.

"What's nice is you are almost done with Ms. Beauty Queen. We have to plan this carefully. No big surprises at the end—from you, buddy. She's one of the best, and she will go quietly."

"About that. I think I may have slipped up, and if she finds out—"

"Well, don't let her find out. Seems pretty simple to me. Got it?"

Xavier looked away. "Not really."

"You're a hot stud. With many bachelor years left in you. Besides, too much money is on the table to risk you being in a real marriage with babies, and all of that. Or messing up this arrangement. Thank God you are filthy rich. Let's keep it that way."

Xavier rose from his seat. He left the office, and never in his life had he felt so empty.

33

———

Thanksgiving sprang up on Candy suddenly. It wasn't a holiday she was used to celebrating, as each of her relationships celebrated differently. She and Cleveland celebrated in a luxury cabin alone in the Swiss Alps, she and Gary at a five-star restaurant in L.A., and this time she found herself lounging on the deck of Xavier's yacht as they sipped wine and ate their meals. Xavier had this last-minute idea to get away on Thanksgiving, and she didn't resist.

"Julio makes these scallops like nobody else," Xavier said as he dabbed his mouth with the napkin. The setting sun painted orange and purple hues on the horizon, and the gentle sea breeze cooled their bodies.

"Perfect, as usual," Candy said as she scooted next to him.

He put his arms around her. "I can get used to this. Used to *us*."

Candy turned to him. "You know, we don't have much time left."

"I know," he sighed, "which got me thinking."

"About what?"

"I can see myself with you beyond this contract. I mean, I would do it if you wanted to stay with me longer. I know the contract doesn't say—"

"It could be worked out," Candy said, delighted to hear his words. "But are you sure?"

"What do you think?"

Candy wanted to say yes, yet she thought about the importance of being professional. The life they built was secure, controlled, and predictable. But was it what she wanted?

He pressed his lips against hers. "Have I done everything I can for you?"

"You've made me realize that I can love again. That it is okay to not be a hundred percent in control, a hundred percent of the time." But she wasn't giving Xavier all the credit for that. A picture of Cleveland came to her mind. He was the only man she wasn't bound to on paper but by heart. Yet Xavier had grown on her in the last several months. She wanted to make sure they ended well.

They kissed some more on the deck, until they made their way downstairs to enjoy the other guests. Elena, Michael, and another couple waited by the stateside bar.

"Here's a Thanksgiving toast," Xavier said as they all gathered at the end of the evening. "I want to thank my beautiful wife, Candy, for everything. For making me the best man I am today," he said as he and everyone else looked at Candy.

"And—and I want to make a toast," Elena said, shooting up her hand.

Candy looked over her shoulder at Elena, slipping by her and grabbing the mic. She beamed at Elena, knowing she'd have something good to say based on her enthusiasm.

"I want to thank my best friend, Candy, for being my everything. You have really helped me find myself again. And Michael," Elena looked over at him, who cut his eyes away, "thank you, too. You know we have stuff to work out, but we will," she mumbled. Then she spoke up again, "And to Xavier. I am working with a whole new director now, Matt Stevens, on a different set. And I want to thank you, Xavier, for being a great boss." Candy and the others clapped and clinked their glasses.

Candy approached Elena. "When did you start working with Matt?"

"Xavier didn't tell you? I started a few weeks ago."

"Is that why you have been MIA?"

"The schedule is crazy. Crazier than Xavier," Elena said. "Oh, let me see what Michael wants. He's mad because we let the kids spend Thanksgiving without us. They're at his mother's." Elena walked away.

Candy was puzzling over the news when Xavier appeared at her side. "Hey, I didn't tell you because I wanted Elena to tell you. Like a surprise. It's really a promotion. Plus, she doesn't get to deal with my crazy mood swings on set anymore," he said, pulling her into his embrace.

"But Elena is my friend. That I referred. You could have told me," Candy said, raising her eyebrows. "Why did you shift her so suddenly?"

"Well," he whispered, "Alfre is working with Matt, and she requested her. So, I told her, instead of going back and forth, work for Matt. It just made sense."

Candy listened, but inside she felt something had been left out.

34

———————

"Time flies," Candy said a few weeks later. Only a month remained on the contract. She sat in Elena's apartment as they caught up. She found Elena's new apartment with its paisley yellow curtains, wooden kitchen cabinets, and brown leather sofa warm and welcoming. They were in sharp contrast to Xavier's home, which was more akin to a luxury hotel lobby.

"Well..." Candy felt stifled by the small talk. She studied Elena. Her whole demeanor shifted more in recent months. Her Botox-pumped cheekbones were more prominent, her dark hair lightened with shades of blonde, and her behind rounder. "You and Michael working things out?"

Elena clenched her teeth and poured herself another glass of juice.

"How about some champagne instead?" Candy said, taking the bottle they had opened, getting ready to pour some.

"No," Elena said, holding her stomach.

Candy flashed a look at her.

"We have to talk, Candy."

"I know. I've been waiting for you to tell me what is going with you lately. Are you okay?"

Elena sat up tall in her chair. "I am more than okay."

Candy took a swig from her glass. But it felt like a boulder hit her stomach.

"Xavier," Elena announced coldly.

"What about him?" Candy sat back.

Elena adjusted the waist to her jeans as she made herself more comfortable on the couch. Her long, thin fingers bought the glass of juice to her lips. "I don't want to cause any drama for you. I can be too friendly sometimes, too," Elena said, putting her hands in the air. "I'll admit that."

"Elena, you know we go way back. With what I do, I can't have many friends. I trust you, and you can trust me. Whatever it is, you can tell me."

Elena bought her hand to wipe away a sudden burst of mascara-coated tears that ran down her cheeks.

Candy moved to sit closer to Elena.

"I do have something to tell you, Candy." Elena grabbed a tissue and wiped her nose. "I did something."

Candy's eyes narrowed, and her throat felt dry, hollow.

"I've been seeing somebody. Well, if you want to call it that…"

Whatever Elena wanted to say was hurting her to say it, yet her tone had an edge that threw Candy off.

"Elena, you know, I can't judge anyone. Is this someone you met at work?"

"Yes."

"How come I never heard about him?"

Elena's shoulders slumped. "I didn't want to upset you."

"And why would I be upset?"

"You know him."

For the life of her, she didn't know why Elena was spoon-feeding her this news. Then Candy laughed nervously as a terrible thought dawned on her.

Elena looked at her with eyes that said it all. "I'm sorry," she said in a whimper.

Candy's entire body felt covered in sweat. "Who is it?" she asked, her voice shaking.

Elena turned her back to Candy and said, "Xavier."

Candy hopped out of her chair and slapped Elena hard across the face, knocking one of her earrings off. "You and Xavier?"

Elena backed away and covered her face. She couldn't bear to look at Candy. "I'm so sorry."

"You're kidding me, right? Please say so," Candy begged. "Please!"

Elena cried loudly.

Candy walked over and pressed her finger against Elena's forehead. "Listen, bitch. You are not going to play the victim here. You plotted against me. Probably from day one." Candy fumed, breathing through her nose. She continued prodding her forehead with her finger until Elena fell back.

"Stop it!" Elena yelled back. "You have everything. Everything! You can get another man like Xavier. What about me?"

Candy stood over her as Elena struggled to stand.

"Bitch, stay there!" Candy said, her heart racing as she contemplated beating Elena down to a bloody mess. "I'll break your neck if you stand up, bitch."

Elena sat on the ground, her knees to her chest, crying into them.

"Tell me what happened!"

Elena shivered. She told her everything. When it began, the day at the pool when they first met. The extended hours on the set when he was really with her, the long phone conversations on the phone on his way home. As Candy listened, it all made sense to her. It explained his late hours, the sudden yacht trips and renewed commitment because he was paranoid about his mess. Candy had a mind to launch into a full-on rage. Today, though, she didn't have it in her. She knew she had to contend with Xavier. But Elena was all she really had in this world. And that, their friendship, was gone.

"And when were you planning on telling me?" Candy said, blocking Elena from standing.

"Candy, why do you care? Your marriage with him is not even real."

"Get up!" Candy said, dragging Elena by her hair until she stood. "You are pathetic. Fuck everything about you. I'm done. We are done. And," Candy said, face to face with Elena, "I am not going anywhere. Hired or not, I am his wife."

"I'm pregnant," Elena said. The words rolled off her tongue.

Candy lost her breath at that moment.

"What I feel is real for Xavier. Can you say that?"

Candy breathed in deeply. "Trapping Xavier will never make you me."

Candy grabbed her bag and bolted out of Elena's apartment, hopped in her car, and drove off. Once she had driven far enough away, she collapsed in grief on the highway.

35

———————

Candy couldn't get Elena off her mind. It frightened her that she could know someone for that long and still not know them. She wondered about the secrets people kept. The lives people led, right in front of her, that she had no idea about. She wondered if that was what she was like, too. The glow she had noticed about Elena the last few months bought it all together. Before Xavier got home, Candy rummaged through his clothes and his cell phones. He had three, two he traveled with and one he left at home as a backup. Candy opened the one at home, lying on the third shelf of his closet, but the voicemail was empty.

A half hour later, she heard Xavier come home. She knew it would take him a few minutes to come upstairs. She decided to play asleep in bed to give herself time to digest everything. She listened as he walked up the steps, called her name, and walked into the bedroom. He stood near the bed to watch her, and she stayed as still as she could.

"You awake?" she heard him ask.

She didn't blink an eye.

He undressed, showered, and threw on a pair of sweats and a shirt. He headed back downstairs for dinner. When he was good and gone, Candy saw one of the work phones. There it was. Texts from Elena, phone calls, and what not. Candy couldn't bring herself to read all of the texts. Her stomach immediately knotted. She raced to the bathroom to throw up. What Elena had confessed was all definitely true. But she wouldn't bring it up to him today, or even tomorrow. She had to plan well. Very well. She put on her best face and joined him for dinner.

~

A FEW WEEKS went by before Candy hatched her plan. With just days left on the contract, and New Year's around the corner, her payout was due. Once she received it, she planned to leave. Yet her heart felt smaller, weak, like a tiny shell inside her. She hadn't eaten in days and lost several pounds. Even Greta's lattes weren't enough. But she didn't want to lay around until Xavier asked what was wrong. He knew she wasn't herself, and she had to bring it to the table.

During breakfast on Saturday morning, Candy felt it was time. She savored her last few cappuccinos made by Greta, who seemed to pour more generously. Almost like she knew the era was ending.

"Thank you, Greta," she said as she sipped her second cup.

"For you, Mrs. Oshun, anything," she said in her syrupy Italian accent.

"Thanks, Greta, you have been so kind to me. I know it's a part of your job, but I know a genuine spirit when I see one."

"Yes, ma'am. Mr. Oshun is very lucky. And I maybe should not to say this, but I know you are leaving us soon. If you ask me, I think you are doing good in the world. You are helping men understand what women need. You are helping women ask for what they need. Mr. Oshun never give to anybody anything. Since you, he give me bonuses, I help my family. I am in a better place because of you. So is my family."

"Oh, Greta." Candy's heart warmed. "That means so much to me."

Greta smiled back, then quickly straightened as Xavier walked in the room. "Good morning, Mr. Oshun."

"Good morning back," he grumbled. Greta walked out the room to prepare his plate. She returned again in a few minutes.

As they ate, Xavier excused himself from the table when his cell rang.

"Who was that?" Candy asked before he sat down again. She pushed her plate to the side.

Xavier's face caved in. "Candy, Elena told me what happened. I just didn't know what to say. I wanted to give you space."

"Told you what?"

"She told you everything."

"And don't you feel you owe me an explanation?"

Xavier covered his face with his hands in defeat.

"And she's pregnant. In case you've been chatting about that, too." Candy leaped out of her chair and charged in his direction. "Look at me." She grabbed his face and turned it toward her. "She's pregnant. You know what this means."

"No, I don't! I didn't plan this," he said, his eyes wide. He reached for her. "You gotta hear me out. Please."

"Get off me," she said, crossing her arms.

"It happened when she invited me to her place. We had sex. And yes, we did it a few times. But she made it seem like it was nothing. Like you'd be okay with it."

"You both deserve each other," Candy said, spinning around. Xavier grabbed her and pulled her toward him. "You can't leave, Candy."

"Like hell, I can't. One thing I ask in all my agreements is respect, Xavier. Without it, there's nothing." Candy couldn't fight back her tears.

He took a few steps back. "I don't know what love is, Candy. I fucked up. Big. But this doesn't have to be the end."

Candy looked up at the ceiling, as if for an escape. She took a deep breath as Xavier wiped her tears. "I'm sorry, Candy. Elena and I met in a real way. It's different."

Candy exhaled. "Yeah, it's different," she whispered.

"I honestly thought maybe you'd help me fix this, too," he said, looking at her. She shook her head. "Xavier, what I can do for you is to leave you alone, per the contract. As soon as I get my payout in the next few days, you won't ever hear from me again."

Xavier's eyes narrowed. "Candy, I can't give you the payout."

"Xavier, that is in the contract. You owe me."

Xavier shifted his feet. He scratched his head. "What about the exit clauses?"

"It doesn't apply here."

Xavier face turned cold, and he said, "Take me to court."

"Xavier, you will pay me. You would not have gotten this far without me."

"That may be right. But if you're going to be a wife, then act like one."

"I did everything you asked of me and things you didn't know how to ask."

"I paid you to be a professional and you leave me at the first sign of indiscretion?"

Candy couldn't believe the turnaround in his attitude, which hurt the most. "People said you couldn't handle this, and they were right. Elena is my best friend. Did you even think about me? But you still have the audacity to lie next to me in bed."

"If you leave me now, you're not getting a dime."

"This is one mess you are going to have to clean up yourself." Candy said, going upstairs. As much as she wanted to leave, she knew she would stay in the house until she figured out how to get around any clause that would allow Xavier to avoid paying.

Because he *was* going to pay.

36

Candy spent New Year's in a separate wing of Xavier's home. He had been spending most of his time with Elena at her place, but that wouldn't last forever. Word about a cheating scandal in their marriage was getting out in the press already. It was messy, and her reputation had always been clean. Xavier was getting ahead of it. What she learned as a professional, all these years, was to stay silent. Stay in control. Let it all go away. But it wasn't.

Candy racked her brain on how she got here. Had Elena planned this all along? Was she always planning this? Her heart filled with rage at Elena. She didn't know if the fact that Elena was white or that Xavier cheated on her with her best friend enraged her most. One of the reasons she was pulled to Xavier was his commitment to marry Black, and be seen with a Black woman. It gave their marriage a vision, a mission they could share together. That all seemed to be for show, a product of his parents' demands probably, she thought. Kids. She wondered if he really wanted kids, making Elena look more desirable, since that was a major no in their contract. Then Elena, who did nothing to get here on her own, swooped in to seize the prize. Elena reminded her of the she-wolves at the Bright Hope gala that night, the she-wolves that would patiently wait and devour anything on their path to get to the meat.

Xavier seemed fake to her now, even dangerous, as he lied straight to her face and then discarded her at the end, threatening her dignity. But she vowed she'd never lose her dignity or self-respect. Her body felt too weak to cry. Her bank account hurt. Xavier's payout would have changed everything for her. She would have never had to work again as a professional wife.

The prospect of marriage with another high-profile man exhausted her, but that was necessary to secure her future. Plus, she was older, and most high-profile men would want children. Her business was competitive, and youth was a valuable asset, along with fertility, as some professional wives only married to give the man a child. But Candy wanted more from her life. A real marriage before any children, a real commitment. Her heart ached to be loved.

She let loose with a wail from the crevices of her soul, loud enough it frightened her. It was like she was hearing a deranged version of herself. She dragged her body to the kitchen and pulled out a bottle of vintage whiskey. She poured and drank down a shot, then another. She flipped open her laptop and saturated herself in Xavier news. There was a recent story, "Love Back in the Air—Xavier Moves on With New Bombshell." A photo of Elena splayed across Xavier on an exotic beach that looked like Cabo, dressed in a white bikini, shades, and the biggest diamond studs in her ears that Candy had ever seen. She read on. Her pregnancy. Real. Xavier. Ecstatic. Joyful. True love.

She slammed the computer shut and took a generous swig of whiskey. Savoring the taste on her lips, she took another. She opened a cabinet in the back of another cabinet in the kitchen, where Xavier kept a gun. She used a chair for leverage, slightly dizzy. She reached in the back of the cabinet to see if it was still there. A .25 derringer. Loaded. She stared at it for what felt like forever, until she gripped the cold metal in her hand. Whether it was the gun or the feel of the cold metal, she felt invigorated, in control again. She put the gun in her bag, jumped into her car, and drove faster than ever.

Before she knew it, she parked behind a tree before the driveway. Her head hammered with pain as she watched Xavier and Elena inside from the street. Walking back and forth, frolicking by the window, enjoying champagne. Like they had no worries in the world, despite the people they had hurt. The family broken, the friendship lost, or the children left behind. Candy's eyes glazed over. *God, help me.* She reached for her gun. She told herself she'd ring the door. She knew Greta would open for her, and she'd act normal before blasting both of them. Because they had already killed her.

She cocked her gun. She opened her car door inch by inch until her feet hit the ground. At that moment, a lark fell out of a tree, landing right in front of her. It was then, seeing the tiny lark helpless on the ground, that she realized she could not throw her life away. Not for anyone.

She needed help.

37

Candy and Lettie had a lunch planned today months ago. And she needed it more than ever.

Candy arranged for a driver to pick up Lettie and bring her to The Falls, an exclusive restaurant in Beverly Hills. She liked showing her sister the finer things. Lettie looked exquisite, dressed in all white, fitted jeans, top, and heels, with hints of gold jewelry. Her hair, pulled up in a playful bun, showcased her narrow shoulders and a tightly defined collarbone.

"Looking dark and lovely," Candy said as she arrived at the table, stretching out her arms for a hug. She noticed a brightness in Lettie she hadn't seen for a long time.

"Look who's talking, Ms. America. Where'd you get that beautiful dress? It's like something out of a fashion magazine," Lettie said, touching the delicate patterns and fabric that draped Candy's body. "Is this silk?"

"What do you think?" Candy adjusted her shades, hoping they would hide her red eyes.

Lettie nodded that it was. "I remember you taught me the difference between real and fake silk years ago."

The waiter glided over and politely announced the specials of the day. Lettie ordered crispy prawns, salad, and polenta fries. Candy ordered her favorite, a Vietnamese steak salad that usually filled her up for the day. "And extra butter, please, for the bread," she said, which was still warm. She tore off a piece.

The waiter thanked them and quickly walked away with their orders.

"Sis, you seem a little distant," Lettie said.

Candy slipped off her shades.

Lettie covered her mouth. She got out of her chair and put her arms around Candy.

Relieved of the pressure to perform like all was well, Candy said, "It's over. In a bad, bad way."

Lettie reached for her sister's hand. "Do you want to talk about it? I may not understand everything. But I'll try."

Candy contemplated whether she should tell her sister or not. She thought that she needed someone to talk to. She decided to go for it.

"Elena slept with Xavier. They both snuck around behind my back. There was nothing in the contract that gave either of us permission to have sex with others. Nothing," she said.

"Candy," Lettie gasped, holding her mouth again. "I'm so sorry. I don't claim to understand everything about that you do. But there must be something about common decency. *That* shouldn't have to be in a contract."

Candy slathered the last of the butter on her bread. "I couldn't agree more."

"But can I say something?"

Candy chewed her bread, relishing the warmth it bought her empty tummy.

"I never liked Elena."

Candy nearly choked on the piece in her mouth.

"Since the day I met her. She always seemed so possessive of you. Anyone that possessive has to be jealous. But I'm sure she played it off like she cared."

Candy listened, thinking to herself the many ways Elena guarded their relationship. She never seemed too far away.

"But now, with Xavier? She's just plain evil and selfish. They both are."

"I thought Elena cared more about our friendship than anything else. She had the *real* thing. Something I never had."

"Let them have each other. Karma takes care of it in the end."

Candy flashed a look at Lettie, pleasantly surprised at her little sister's shrewdness.

"And, from where I sit, *you* are the real thing," Lettie added.

Candy inhaled deeply, as her sister hugged her across the table.

"Let's focus on you," Candy said, feeling a sense of relief. "So, are you going to fill me in? I know Mommy had something to say when I left last time."

"Strangely, she didn't."

Candy tilted her head to the side.

"I actually think you gave her a lot to think about last time."

"Seriously?"

"Seriously," Lettie laughed. "No one speaks up to her but you. After you left, I told her that I was moving out. I thought she was going to blow up. But she didn't. She said she didn't want to have two daughters who hated her."

"Go on."

"So, I think she may be finally seeing the effects of the pain we both went through with her, and it is finally hitting her she's going to be alone. There is no way I can live with her anymore."

Candy said, "I'm really proud of you. I know this is hard."

Tears streamed down Lettie's face, and she dabbed them with the tablecloth.

Candy handed her a napkin. "And you're doing it on your own terms. Don't you worry, she will always be taken care of, I'll make sure of it. We'll also have to take turns visiting her."

"Yes, yes, right," Lettie said, finally breaking into a smile. "It may take me a while, though."

"I get it."

Their plates of food came, lavishly displayed and sumptuous. Candy's mouth watered at her salad. She felt even hungrier than when she arrived. As they ate, they both nodded at each other with filled mouths at how fresh and delicious everything tasted.

"You know, Candy," Lettie said, putting down her fork, "I just want to thank you for helping me see what is possible. Paying for me to go full-time really helped. I've caught up so much, and I'm on time for graduation."

"I knew you could do it. And I hope your pre-med boyfriend is motivating you to stay in those books."

Lettie nodded, glad for her sister's approval. They finished their lunches with talk about other matters.

"You know what we have to do now, right?" Candy asked.

Lettie smiled with her eyes.

38

———————

When Candy returned to Xavier's place, a sense of urgency filled her. Everyone was moving on with their lives, and she had to, too. She peered at her reflection in the bathroom mirror, stroking a brush against her cheeks and dotting a few bits of highlighter around her brow and cheeks. She added a few drops of Visine to her eyes. She did her best to chin up. She couldn't explain where she was mentally, but it was a rare place of having no control and not caring. She was relieved and curious about what lay in front of her.

She checked her phone. A beep notified her of a voicemail from Cleveland. "I've been trying to reach you for days, call me." It was time to get Cleveland involved. She normally dealt with his associate, but this was big.

The drive the next day to Cleveland's office was quick, no traffic, unusual for noon in L.A. As she walked toward the building, she bumped into a light-skinned Black woman who looked just like Tisha Campbell from *Martin*.

"Candy?" she said, her smile showing perfectly white teeth.

Candy stopped dead in her tracks. It was Doreen, her former assistant from her fashion days. Candy had the type of job that was so

182

hard that even the assistants had assistants. Doreen had a little brown girl next to her in a red and blue dress that looked no older than seven years old. "Doreen, what ever happened to you? Didn't you move back to New York?"

"I did and then moved right back to L.A. I missed it. The weather, the laid-back vibes. And I also bought something back with me. This is Nicole. Nicole, meet my former boss, Candy."

Nicole waved her little hand back and forth, smiling.

"Hi, honey," Candy said, holding her hand for a light handshake. She noticed that she and Doreen were wearing matching white and beige sneakers. Only Doreen, Candy thought. But before she could comment on it, Doreen kept going.

"And you, miss thang. You can't stay out of the gossip blogs. Are they still called blogs?"

They both laughed. Passersby looked at them as they caught up right outside of Cleveland's building. It was a busy lunch hour with people walking by eating sandwiches or sitting with their salads on nearby benches.

"Candy, you look as beautiful as the day we met almost twenty years ago. You haven't aged a bit. I heard what happened with Xavier Oshun. I have never trusted those African men."

"Now you tell me." Candy tried to laugh.

"He has no idea what he lost. I cannot support Black men who marry white women. They are the biggest traitors. They talk about helping the race and then sleep with the enemy. Right, girl?"

"Yeah, Doreen." Candy flashed a fake smile. She knew she could not reveal much at all about her marriage or lifestyle.

"That's it? I would take that man for every dime he has—"

"Doreen—" Candy started to change the subject.

"—I will never watch another Xavier Oshun movie again. All his interviews about positive Black love were just fake. Can I ask one question, though?"

"Actually —"

"Why Elena? I didn't understand what you both had in common. I always thought she was one of those parasites. Those people who latch onto other people, until they become those people, or eat them alive."

"You know what, Doreen," Candy responded, "I never asked myself about Elena. She never gave me a reason to. She had her own husband."

"Those be the ones," she said, leaning in. She covered her daughter's ears slightly, as if she had done it before. "They use their husbands as fronts to disarm other women. Would y'all had been friends so long if she wasn't married?"

Candy hadn't seen it that way before. She looked around, as she noticed a pap across the street taking a photo. She turned slightly. "Probably not."

Doreen snapped her fingers. "Exactly." She gave Candy a once-over, from her designer heels up to the turquoise and diamond pendent necklace set on her flawless skin. "You are in a class all by yourself, baby."

"Thank you, Doreen. And from the looks of it, you're not doing too bad yourself. What's been going on with you?"

"I had Nicole with one of my exes. She's my miracle baby. No ring yet."

"Grant Marshall?" Candy said, recalling the acclaimed former Green Bay Packers receiver.

Doreen nodded as they caught up on her own life. Doreen was ten years older than Grant, making her fifty years old. Candy did the math in her head quickly and felt connected to Doreen being an older, single mom. Candy thought that took a lot of guts.

"Can we stay in touch?" Candy heard herself asking. She had never imagined needing a friend more than she did now.

"Sure," Doreen said as they both took out their cell phones. "We go to church on Sundays, too. If you ever want to join us."

"That sounds nice," Candy said.

"Actually, that's my Uber now to pick us up." Doreen waved at the driver. "Candy, it was so nice seeing you again. Promise me you'll take care, okay? Call me."

"I will," Candy said, adjusting her shades on her nose as Doreen and her daughter climbed into the car.

Candy made her way up to Cleveland's office. She waited. Waiting for Cleveland's brilliant ideas to get her out of this mess, or waiting for Cleveland. Ever since their marriage ended, the men she met never matched up. Or was it supposed to be that way. Was he supposed to be the one that did?

A receptionist greeted her and escorted her to Cleveland's office.

"Good morning," Candy said in a confident tone, not wanting to give off any airs of worry.

Cleveland stood up, walked over, and grabbed her hands for a kiss. "Good morning," he said, settling down on a chair across from her own. "So, we have a lot to discuss," he said, his arms folded.

"It's over," she said.

"I heard," he sighed.

"Go ahead, say it," Candy said, slowly slipping off her shades.

"I told you about men like Xavier. You can't trust them. Those guys come into these entertainment circles hungry. Sloppy—"

"He was already accomplished in his own right. I just thought he was different."

"You're still in the house?" Cleveland pulled out a copy of her contract.

"Yes."

"Good. If you had left, it would be considered abandonment of the agreement. You make sure you stay there."

"Oh, I will," Candy said. "Nobody is going to scare me off this easily."

Cleveland slipped on his eyeglasses and poured over the papers for the next few minutes. He took them off and leaned back in his chair. "This is some iron-clad shit. I'm impressed."

Candy looked on, not sure if that was good or bad.

"But with everything he is putting you through, you should be compensated fully." He slipped off his glasses. "And Elena?"

That name made her cringe.

"If I know you, Candy, Elena doing this to you hurts more than Xavier."

A tear slid down from Candy's eye. Cleveland handed her a tissue. "That part hurts just a little more. I trusted her with everything. I helped her when she needed me most. But," she said, her eyes narrowing as she spoke, "I messed up, too. I let her in. I got her the job. I made it easy."

Cleveland came around his desk and sat in the chair next to her. He took her hand and held it. She squeezed it as they both stared out the glass window in front of them, off in their own thoughts.

"I don't have many friends myself, Candy. Yes, I know a lot of people. But when we choose a different life from ninety-nine percent of the population, we have fewer relationships to choose from. That means choosing wisely or not choosing at all."

"Well, I rather not for a while. I'm good alone."

Cleveland's eyes canvassed her, as if he wanted to say more. But he did not want to silence her feelings. He thought it was important to hear her out.

"This is not about just getting paid. This is the fact that my whole life I have spent helping people. Getting people what they want. Getting people ahead. Everyone is going off to have their fulfilled lives built off my graces. And what do I get?" She looked at Cleveland.

"You get a heart that's still beating. Still believing in love. Do you?"

"It gets smaller every day. I just don't want to grow bitter. I feel like that tree in that story. Where everyone ate the fruit, leaving the tree by itself in the end."

Cleveland had never seen Candy so vulnerable. It moved him in an unexpected way he couldn't explain. He wanted to take her out of this whole mess, and he absolutely had to.

Candy stood up, gathering herself. "Thank you, Cleveland," she said, mustering a light smile. "You always have my back."

"Always." He stood up and reached for her. "I see you've grown so much since we met. You've gotten not only benefits of this life, but you are one of the rare people who learned from it and still have their soul intact. I admire you for that. For the care you have for your heart," Cleveland said. "I'm going to divorce Marlene."

Candy wanted to jump for joy but contained herself. "Why now?"

"She's not happy and neither am I. And," he said, taking in a breath. "When I saw your news, I felt it was time. And I think she saw it coming, too."

Candy felt her heard stop in her chest as she held her breath.

"What are *we* doing?" he asked Candy, shaking his head back and forth. "I love you. More and more each time I see you."

"Cleveland, I will always love you. I guess our timing has never been all the way right."

"That, too." He nodded, thinking for a moment. "There are people who eat the fruit from the tree and people who water the tree. You need water."

Candy was on the verge of crying, her shoulders softened. She blew her nose into the tissue as Cleveland held on tight to her.

"And what I mean is," Cleveland said, "you need someone who can pour into you. Settle *you*."

Candy made a small laugh. "I never had that. Except with—"
"With *me*."

"I would have been your wife with or without a contract." She smiled at him, losing herself in his assurance.

"Give me a few weeks. I will work all of this out. *All* of it."

39

"Candy, is that you?" her mother said, walking down the steps with a cigarette in her hand.

Candy only smiled with her mouth closed. She still hated the smell of cigarettes. This afternoon, she wanted some time with her mom. Since her last conversation with Lettie, she knew this was something she had to handle alone.

Her mother put the cigarette out in an ashtray by the window.

"Mommy, we need to talk. I'm not here to fight."

Her mother sat down on the couch without saying a word. That's new, Candy thought. She had already sensed something different.

Her mother scanned her expensive bag and diamond ring, which she still wore. "Are you okay?" she said.

"I will be. I have good people helping me."

"Cleveland?"

"Yes," she replied, her mother's response surprising her.

Her mother's eyebrows raised. "He was always the best of them."

Candy's mouth froze. She had never heard her mother say anything nice about him, but it looked like she had been watching the whole time. She reached in her bra, pulled out an envelope, and handed it to her. "This is what I owe you."

Candy opened it and took a peek. It was a check.

"It's what I owe you. All the time I took your money, never paid as promised, and I took money you didn't know."

Candy stared at the check. She gave it back. Candy looked at her mom with warm eyes. She was lost for words.

"No, please take it. And you don't have to worry about where it came from. I did save some, so some of it is still yours. And Lettie helped me put this together, too." But her mother wasn't done.

Candy put the check in her bag, her hands shaking.

"I treated you like the crap at the bottom of my shoe. You were here from the start. You seen it all. Before Lettie, during, and after. You know what I've been through. We both grew up together. But that is no excuse for what I put you through. How I abandoned you, left you, deserted you. Candy, I was jealous of you. Jealous of your resilience, your courage, your smarts. Your beauty. That you can go out there and take charge of your world. I never could do that." Her mother paused. "How you do that? I may never know. I respect you, nonetheless, and what you had to do to build a life for yourself—and ours. All because I dropped the ball long ago. Thank you for everything you have done. For having a heart for me when I didn't for you. For taking care of me when I can barely take of myself. You gave me what you did not have. I cannot thank you enough."

"Mommy, it's my duty as your daughter. You can never do anything that would make me *not* do that. I couldn't live with myself if I did. Yes, you hurt me. You changed me. It is what it is. Thank you for acknowledging what you couldn't do."

"Thank you, Jesus," her mother said with a sigh of relief.

Candy smiled. God rarely came out of their mother's mouth.

"Mommy, are you okay?"

"I am better than OK. Can you forgive me?"

"Yes, I can," Candy said. "What about Lettie?"

"We're good. I had a long talk with her, too," she said, taking a deep breath.

"Where do we go from here?" Candy asked.

"We can start right here."

"All I ever wanted to hear was what just came out of your mouth," Candy said. "We are all we got. Men come and go, jobs come and go, but we have to stick together. I need you more now than I ever have." Candy was surprised at those last words, but it was true.

"I wish I can explain it to you. I was visited by an angel who showed me what would happen to you two if we didn't make peace. He showed me what happened to me. How I turned into this mean, old surly thing for the last forty years. I woke up, and I felt clear. Like something pulled me awake. I knew what I needed to do."

Candy asked, "What did you see?"

"It doesn't matter. I know now that you both will be fine. I feel like we vanquished a curse or something. Like something broke over this family to make us wake up. Does that make sense?" Candy's mother squeezed both her hands ever so tightly. "Thank you, Jesus," she said, again, tears streaming down her freckled cheeks.

Candy got chills all over hearing her mother's words. "Amen," she muttered as they pulled in for a hug, for the first time in years.

40

Today marked the last official day of Candy's marriage to Xavier. It was late in the evening when the movers were finally done. She had said her goodbyes to Greta and all the helpers earlier in the day. Xavier had been home the entire time and stayed in his office. She preferred it that way.

"Thanks, guys," Candy said, giving her last instructions for the evening. "I will meet you at my house in a few."

As the trucks drove off, Candy looked at the time. It was nine. Dark. She had one more thing she had to do. She walked back inside the house.

In the kitchen, Greta had saved her a whole glass jar of her creamy cappuccino that she could heat up in the morning. She was ever so grateful. As she walked around the dark, quiet home, she heard footsteps. She had no idea Xavier had guests.

A gorgeous, slender woman wandered down the front staircase, dressed in a pink negligee. She had pink-heeled slippers, too.

"Oh, hello," she said to Candy as she sashayed to the kitchen like she had been there before.

Candy stayed until the young woman headed back up the steps again with two wine glasses.

Candy looked up at Xavier, who was waiting at the top of the stairs. "Whoops," he said as he put his arm around the woman.

Her mouth agape, Candy closed the door behind her, seeing things clearly.

A FEW DAYS LATER, Candy closed the accounts at her favorite shops with Brent's help. She had to get her affairs in order. She deposited a check to Lettie, the last one in a while. She'd be graduating at the end of the semester.

"There! I just scheduled your last spa treatment at Jardin. I know you need to be extra-moisturized for your next suitor," Brent quipped as they both sat in Candy's home.

"Please block these sites from my computer." She handed Brent a list.

There seemed to be a new lightness in the fall winds that blew through the open balcony window.

"And you'll be a lot closer to me again! The ride up to you and Xavier was no joke," he said, shaking his head and flipping channels.

"Stop there," Candy said as she spotted Marlene's show. "I want to see this."

"This trash?" Brent said.

"Yes, yes, turn it up." Candy felt drawn to the show this morning. Marlene had a new hair color, but there was no background music.

With each word out of Marlene's mouth, Candy felt a stab in her chest.

Brent looked at her. "I'll turn the channel," he said, reaching for the remote.

"No." Candy gently took it back from him. "Let it finish."

Candy's entire life was blowing up in her face, soundbite by soundbite, photo by photo. Marlene exposed her life like she had every other celebrity on her show. But this time it was with disgust.

"Is it even legal what this woman does?" Marlene asked. "How she manipulates men to marry her? Destroys lives ..."

Candy felt limp all at once, and sat down on the couch.

"How can it be okay to let a man pay you to be his wife?" The audience booed and moaned. "I mean, really, y'all. In this day and age, women are independent, we are strong, we don't need a man to make it out there anymore…"

The audience cheered. One woman stood up and clapped hard.

"Candy Robertson is a swindler, a hustler. She's extorting these men. *Allegedly*."

Brent turned the TV off.

"Brent," Candy said, "Please—"

"No, are you kidding me? Candy, this woman is out to destroy you. Can you file a libel suit?"

Candy closed her eyes. And she considered that option for a moment. She could file a suit, deny it all, and pray her reputation was restored. But then she said, "No."

Brent shot her a worried look.

"What if she is right?"

"Right?" Brent said. "No, ma'am!"

"What if?"

Brent rolled his eyes. "Candy, you have been a help to women, if anything. You have showed that women can set marriage on their own terms. You have showed women how to ask for what they want and get paid for it. Look at all the lives you have changed, charities you started, influence you've had in other people's worlds. You have been in charge of your life, and how many of us can say that?"

Candy listened, struck by his fervor.

"I know about five single women right now who wish they had a man pay them to be their wife. For companionship, a partner in life, someone to sleep with at night. Marriage isn't just about one thing. Hell, most of the world doesn't even marry for love…" he added. "Can we talk about dowries?"

Brent's tirade stopped Candy from the feeling of dread. She smiled at his college professor hat coming back on. "You know what?"

"What?" Brent asked, his eyes growing worried again.

"It's time," Candy said, exhausted from the sound of Marlene's voice. "I'm getting older, and I deserve more than this. More than the money, bright lights, status. I need a partner, a real relationship with someone I deeply love, and who loves me just a tiny bit more."

Brent shook his head up and down. "But what about your lifestyle. You can't just go back to being a civilian."

Candy huffed. "Who would marry me now, Brent? No man wants a woman who does this for his real wife. He'll feel he can never measure up, or worse, trust me." She went on, "I wanted to leave when *I* was ready, and have a plan for taking care of myself." Candy breathed out loudly, stretching her legs out, and laying back on the couch. She just couldn't think anymore.

Brent's deadening silence told Candy all she needed to hear.

"Who would hire me?"

Brent simply shook his head as he looked down at his feet.

"I can't work – ever – now with everyone knowing who I am."

Brent looked at her with pitiful eyes. "Honey, you can't even get a job at the Dairy Queen."

Brent was right. She'd never be able to work in this town again as anything or feel safe with her business out there. She didn't care. Not anymore. She was who she was. She had become a woman as a professional wife and learned invaluable skills that would never make her a victim. She didn't know exactly what lay ahead, but she wanted to help other women. Not on how to get married, but how to never be alone—married or not.

41

Cleveland and Marlene's divorce made the papers for the next few days. But Candy did not let it distract her from her own legal proceedings.

Xavier, dressed in a flawless gray suit and tie, sat with his lawyer, Andrew Goldenblatt, confidently with both of their hands neatly folded on a stack of papers. Xavier exuded confidence, staring her and Cleveland in the eye with a smirk. It was almost like he enjoyed every moment.

Candy made sure she looked her best. Seeing the woman at his house the other night, she was glad to be rid of him. She wore a sleek black Chanel suit and a white blouse with a few of the top buttons loosened. She wasn't going to let Xavier see her shriveled or demure. She was still who she was. Cleveland complemented her style just by his brooding presence.

"My client is not giving up another penny. The agreement is the agreement. Now that Ms. Robertson has left the home, and the marriage is officially over, it is over. We can, however, offer her a year complementary service at her favorite spa," quipped Andrew, an older Jewish man.

"A spa? Is this a joke?" Candy let out a laugh. "Please."

Cleveland gave her a look, hiding his own disbelief. "I have heard enough," he said as Claude gave him a stack of papers. Cleveland put on his glasses, and Candy knew that meant business. She slipped back in her chair. Xavier whispered in his lawyer's ear.

"According to clause 5c, if the husband cheats on her, Candy gets paid. Cash. No spa. No gift certificates. No fifty-dollar coupons."

"She abandoned the home," Andrew asserted.

"Oh, is that what your client said?"

Xavier shifted in his chair. Andrew looked at him, and the contract again. "There is no clause 5c." He looked back at Cleveland.

"I ain't giving her a damn dime," Xavier snarled, cutting his eyes at Candy.

She didn't blink.

Cleveland leaned forward, addressing Xavier's attorney. "He cheated on her. Unless of course, Xavier wants to tell us what he really did to reach his success so soon."

The room got still. Candy perked up.

Xavier's chest fell.

Then Cleveland turned to him. "You remember some photos you took when you were in Bangkok? Some, very, let's say, lewd photos doing things that make you look like the empty vessel you are with a certain provocateur who is in jail now? Should I say more?"

"Fine, Fine, Fine!" Xavier slammed his hand down.

Cleveland said to Andrew in a terse tone, "*He* abandoned the contract. Should we leave it at that?"

Andrew's eyes went from Xavier to Cleveland. "Are you threatening my client?"

"Fuck this!" Xavier said. "Give them what they want. I'm not about to lose my career over this bullshit."

"Excuse me, I didn't hear that," Cleveland said.

Andrew whispered something to Xavier. Then, Xavier pulled out a check, wrote the amount, and slipped it to Andrew. Andrew gave it to Cleveland. "Welp, I guess we are done here. Gentlemen," Andrew said, and left.

Xavier slowly rose from his chair, facing Candy and Cleveland. "I knew you two were conspiring against me this whole time."

"Goodbye, Xavier," Candy said. "And good luck. You are going to need it."

Xavier seemed to shrink even more. They watched him leave.

Candy flew out of her chair as Cleveland handed her the check. "Are there really photos?" she asked.

"Do you really want to know?"

Candy gulped.

"I will always make sure you are taken care of. Ok?"

As they walked together outside and chatted, neither wanted to get into their separate cars. "You know," Candy told him, "what Marlene said on her show has ruined me on the marriage circuit forever or with any kind of job."

Cleveland smiled. "Maybe that isn't a problem. What if I want to take you off the circuit permanently?"

"What do you mean, permanently?" The hair on Candy's skin rose. *Yes, yes.*

"I want to marry you," he said as he held her in front of his office building.

Their bodies touched in a way that Candy never experienced before. Electric bolts shot through her. She said, "You are who I always wanted. If it took what I been through to get here with each other, it's been worth all the husbands."

EPILOGUE

A YEAR AND SOME MONTHS LATER

"Aren't we too young to be retired?" Candy asked Cleveland as they lay on the beach in their new home in Barbados. Candy relaxed in a hammock, admiring the blue, choppy waves in front of her. Cleveland, in the other hammock, reached over and rubbed her belly. She was six months pregnant. They remarried nine months ago, just after everything ended with Marlene.

A light breeze snatched her sun hat off her head. Cleveland went after it.

As she watched him, she could not get over how they were so settled, a regular couple. A married couple. No term contracts. Everything felt possible from this point on. And he was an exceptional husband. He showered her with the love, protection, and attention she thrived on. Settled, yes. In her fullness, finally.

Lettie had moved in with her pre-med boyfriend, who now had a residency at a local hospital. Candy sold her mother's house. They all agreed that it was too big for one person anymore. Her mother got a part-time job at a local store and was finally supporting herself. Candy felt good that her mother would be okay, and she could still help her – on her terms – if she needed it. Cleveland was generous that way. Needless to say, he and her mom got along, too.

Once Cleveland handed back her hat, Candy flipped through one of her gossip rags.

"Look at this," she said, handing to him.

He read it. "What's worse than payback? Backpay," he said.

Elena and Xavier were no longer together. She had the baby without him. He was in a new contract with an alcohol rehab center for ninety days. Candy wished him the best. She harbored no bitterness for either of them. Well, maybe some for Elena. She would never understand why she sacrificed their friendship. But as she looked down at the budding life within her, she felt her new life was priceless.

JOIN THE VIP CLUB

Want more? It doesn't have to end here.

Stay connected to Maryann Reid for updates, free giveaways, and exclusive invitations directly from the author at maryannreidinc.com.

READING GROUP DISCUSSION GUIDE

General questions

- What major emotional response did the story evoke in you?
- Did the book take you outside your comfort zone?
- What question do you think the author was trying to find an answer to?
- Can a "professional wife" be a real wife?
- Is being a "professional wife" a viable option? What if you knew the end date of your relationship in advance?
- Do you think Xavier and Candy would have been together if they met under different circumstances?

Character questions

- How do you think Candy grew from the beginning to the end of the story?
- Were there any characters you loved to hate?

- Was Candy's reaction to the news of what happened with Elena justified?
- Xavier almost seemed like the perfect guy. How does being a good/bad boy make him more/less attractive?
- How did you feel about Cleveland hanging on to Candy? Were they meant to be from the start?
- Why do you think Elena was Candy's friend? Was it to be like her or something more?
- Marlene is opinionated and an adversary. How is she and Candy alike/different?

Character decisions

- Candy's family is estranged in many instances. Do you think Candy handled those moments right?
- According to Candy's sister Lettie, she never liked Elena. Was this just jealousy or more you think?
- Candy's mother chose a surprising route in the end. What do you think prompted this?
- Candy chose her men based on certain criteria. Why do you think Xavier was important at this point in her life?
- Candy overlooks warnings about Xavier's behavior. What do you think other women would think of her decision?

Social issues

- Attitudes to marriage have changed drastically over the last 100 years. What advantages/disadvantages did Candy's chosen lifestyle have over women today?
- At a time when men and women disagree on many things, how does Candy use her position of power in the marriage to her advantage?
- In a culture where marriage is defined in several ways, how does Candy redefine marriage as a whole?

- Cleveland is the proverbial father figure looking out for Candy. Does he help or hinder Candy's growth into the woman she eventually becomes?
- The wives in Candy's world are aware of their power and what they give/get, what can other women learn from this?

Closing questions

- What did the title come to mean to you by the end of the novel?
- Were you satisfied with the book's ending? What do you think the future holds for Candy?
- Did the novel leave any questions open that you would have liked to have the answer to?
- Do you think Lettie will follow in Candy's shoes? Why/why not?
- If you had to halve the size of your book collection, would this book stay or go?
- If you could ask the author a question, what would it be?

Schedule a book club discussion
with the author at www.maryannreidinc.com.